A Wedding in Valentine

Also by Emma Cane

True Love at Silver Creek Ranch
A Town Called Valentine

A Wedding in Valentine

A VALENTINE VALLEY NOVELLA

EMMA CANE

AVONIMPULSE
An Imprint of HarperCollinsPublishers

Excerpt from *The Cowboy of Valentine Valley* copyright © 2014 by Gayle Kloecker Callen.

Excerpt from *A Town Called Valentine* copyright © 2012 by Gayle Kloecker Callen.

Excerpt from *True Love at Silver Creek Ranch* copyright © 2013 by Gayle Kloecker Callen.

Excerpt from *The Cupcake Diaries: Sweet On You* copyright © 2013 by Darlene Panzera.

Excerpt from *The Cupcake Diaries: Recipe for Love* copyright © 2013 by Darlene Panzera.

Excerpt from *The Cupcake Diaries: Taste of Romance* copyright © 2013 by Darlene Panzera.

Excerpt from *One True Love* copyright © 2013 by Laurie Vanzura.

EPub Edition JUNE 2013 ISBN: 9780062264657

Print Edition ISBN: 9780062264664

JV 10 9 8 7 6 5 4 3 2 1

To Michele Masarech, longtime friend and fellow Packeteer: A love of writing brought us together, and I'll always be thankful, because I depend on your humor, caring, and advice—and traveling is just not as fun without you!

Chapter One

HEATHER ARMSTRONG GASPED as the plane dropped down between the Colorado mountains, which were painted a myriad of greens below the tree line, barren and brown at the top, awaiting the next winter's snow. The ground seemed to rush up, and only when they touched down at the small Aspen airport did she let her exhilaration at her first mountain landing subside back into wedding excitement. She was about to be a bridesmaid in the June wedding of an old friend, Emily Murphy.

As she waited for a call from Emily, she wandered the small airport. It bustled with people dressed casually for the outdoors, many carrying cases for fishing equipment, a pastime this valley was known for in the summer. She'd always preferred being a people watcher, a person in the background rather than commanding attention to herself. It was one of the reasons she'd never enjoyed being in charge of a restaurant's kitchen, and had opened her own catering business. But now her people-watching skills made her halt in her tracks as she caught a glimpse of a familiar face.

A man wearing a cowboy hat slouched in a chair near the main doors, as if he, too, was waiting for someone. With his head bent over a book, she couldn't quite see his face. A feeling of unease shivered up her spine and made her so wary that she backed up to where she was partially hidden around the corner. Peeking out again, she studied his pale blond hair beneath the hat, the checked Western shirt that snugly outlined his broad chest, the long legs encased in faded jeans above worn cowboy boots.

The bang of dropped luggage drew his attention, and he looked up. Heather recognized him instantly, and with a gasp, she retreated behind the safety of the wall. His name was Chris, and that was all she'd known when they'd been snowbound together in the Denver airport seven months ago. Late night drinks at the bar and mutual attraction—make that lust—shared with Chris had turned her into a person she'd never been before, a daring flirt who'd ended up in bed with a cowboy. They'd spent two wild days together, exploring and laughing and connecting on an intimate level that had surprised her with its depth, considering they'd been strangers and all. Though she'd left him her number, assuming they'd see each other again, he'd never called. She'd felt like an idiot, a slut, and whatever other bad names she'd called herself over the following months.

Gradually she'd accepted the "adventure" as a risk she'd obviously wanted to take, and had learned from.

She wasn't cut out for one-night stands. She felt too much, expected too much. A man pursuing such a brief affair wanted only that and nothing else.

Today had been the first day airports hadn't made her think about him, she thought bitterly. Tough luck for her.

To find some peace, she'd chalked the experience up to a valuable lesson. Other women had done stupid things in college, but not her. She'd been too focused on her business degree, and then culinary school, the future her goal, little lured by frat parties and wild drinking. She'd had a boyfriend or two, of course, serious engineering or business students, and that same pattern had continued throughout most of her twenties. Never time for an intense relationship—until Andrew, four years before. She'd thought everything so perfect, so wonderful, and hadn't even seen that he was pulling away from her, that their sex life was full of desperation more than real passion. Everything on the surface had been too good to be true. The breakup with him was probably what had launched her desperation that snowy night in Denver.

But Chris's face had haunted her a long time, lean and sculpted, his blue eyes almost startling in their intensity. She hadn't been with another man since him, had been ready to change her life, find a new place to start over, all to forget her past and find more peaceful surroundings.

Heather had always thought *she'd* be the first one to give up the hectic, stressful pace of the city, not Emily. She'd gone to San Francisco for culinary school, and to make a name for herself, eventually establishing her own catering business. She came from a small town herself, but her own mountain town in California would never be able to support a fulltime catering business. Emily had assured her that Valentine Valley could. And who could resist a name like Valentine?

But was seeing Chris some kind of cosmic sign that a move here wasn't for her? She didn't believe in that sort of stuff, but still found herself praying that he was just passing through Aspen . . .

And then Emily Murphy walked through the outer doors, strawberry-blond hair bobbing in a ponytail, a bright yellow sundress matching the brilliance of her smile framed in her heart-shaped face. And why shouldn't she smile? She was the bride, about to marry her very own cowboy, Nate Thalberg. Heather felt tender affection relax her own worried expression, and she scolded herself for her panicky thoughts. She would find a way to avoid Chris and a possible scene. She wouldn't do anything to disrupt Emily's weekend.

But to her dismay, Chris rose to his feet and enfolded Emily in a big hug. *They knew each other?* Heather thought with disbelief. From her cowardly hiding place, she could hear their conversation.

"I thought you wanted me to pick up your friend?" Chris said.

Emily shrugged. "I know, but I got some things done and I just couldn't wait. You don't mind your big sister dropping in, do you?"

Big sister? Heather focused on those words in shock. She'd known Emily had found her biological father and stepmother in Valentine Valley, and more than once she'd mentioned her new siblings, but mostly Stephanie, the teenager who hadn't been exactly happy to meet Emily.

And then Heather covered her mouth as realization dawned. She'd confessed her fling to Emily, having needed to confide in someone—what would Emily say if she found out her own brother was the mystery man? Not that Heather had given her any details like where or when. That had seemed too private even to share with a best friend. Heather didn't know if she could live down the embarrassment, nor could she stand the thought of destroying their friendship if Emily took it badly—and on her wedding weekend, too!

Emily gave Chris a curious tilt of the head. "So how did you plan to recognize Heather?"

"Well, you said she was a redhead. How could I miss?" He grinned when Emily put her hands on her hips skeptically. "Naw, really, I brought a sign with her name on it. It's folded in my book somewhere."

"You and your books," she teased. "She might have walked right past you."

"I was being careful."

Their conversation faded as Heather stiffened her shoulders with resolve. Her plans for a relaxing weekend were shot out the window, and there was nothing to do but grit her teeth and bear it for Emily's sake—and her own. She hoped it wouldn't be difficult to convince Chris to keep their affair a secret. Surely he cared about his sister's feelings. She prayed he'd keep his thoughts to himself until they had a chance to talk in private.

And as for how he'd treated Heather herself? She

wasn't going to show this thoughtless cowboy that he'd hurt her by not calling. She'd make it perfectly clear that she was a worldly woman of the big city, who understood how unimportant a fling was.

If only she *was* that sort of woman ... if only the thought of Emily being upset about their relationship didn't unnerve her. She'd never do anything to risk losing her friendship—but now it looked like she'd already risked everything.

She couldn't hide forever, she thought, taking a deep, cleansing breath to steady her nerves. Adjusting the large purse on her shoulder, she started to walk, pulling her suitcase behind. She felt like the entire airport was staring; instead it was just Chris who noticed her first. She couldn't read his expression, but experienced the magnetism of his blue eyes as if she were back in biology class, a butterfly pinned to a display board on the teacher's wall.

Did he recognize her? Did his heartbeat speed up like hers did—like hers *had* the first time she'd seen him in the Denver baggage area, trying to persuade a shuttle to drive through a rising snowstorm from the nearest hotel? His voice had been commanding but polite, and he'd at last won the operator over with easygoing cowboy charm, though she'd seen the tension in his fisted hands. The discrepancy had fascinated her, and she'd found her gaze constantly returning to him, as she waited in line to use the same hotel phone. And then he'd smiled at her, and she was lost. Now, months later, he was looking at her again, inspiring a mass of conflicting emotions: anger, hurt, and the undercurrent of desire that still flamed just as strong.

Emily must have realized Chris was looking past her shoulder, and she turned, her smile widening when she saw Heather. With a squeal, Emily opened her arms wide for a hug. After letting go of her suitcase, Heather enjoyed the temporary respite of being enfolded in Emily's warmth and caring.

"I'm so glad you're here!" Emily said, taking a step back, but still squeezing Heather's upper arms.

"Me, too," Heather answered, her attention firmly focused on her friend rather than the looming man behind Emily. "I can't believe you're getting married!"

"And in two days! I feel like there's so much to do, but that's just panic, I think. Nate says I need to calm down and enjoy the festivities, and of course, he's right." Emily laughed at herself. "Oh, and you may be wondering about this handsome guy behind me. I asked him to come get you, but then I was able to get away, too, so here we both are. Heather Armstrong this is my brother, Chris Sweet."

And then Heather was forced to meet his eyes again, and she didn't know how she kept up her polite smile. She was just as captivated as the first time, but if she was waiting for—dreading—an answering smolder of awareness, she got nothing, only a friendly smile in return. She swallowed hard, not knowing whether to be confused or grateful that he didn't spill out the truth. *Oh, I've met Heather before. Let me tell you the whole story . . .*

"Nice to meet you, Heather," Chris said, in that deep cowboy drawl that had once made her melt right on her bar stool when they'd decided to get a drink to pass the long snowbound evening.

She broke eye contact and chirped, "You, too!" She smiled at Emily, trying to smother her nervousness. She wasn't the kind of woman used to hiding secrets—which is why she'd confessed the fling. She wished she could link arms with Emily and march out of there, leaving Chris in the dust, but she wouldn't be so impolite. "Thanks for offering to pick me up."

"No problem," he said, giving his hat a polite tug.

Emily gave her brother a quick hug. "I'll let you head back to the ranch. Are you coming to the party tonight?"

"Of course."

Emily had sent a schedule ahead, so Heather knew exactly what they were talking about—a co-ed bachelor/bachelorette party. She'd probably see Chris Sweet at every single event over the weekend. She could have groaned. With her luck, they'd be paired up walking down the aisle!

"I'll leave you two girls to chat," Chris said. "See you later."

Had that been directed right at her? Heather wondered. But she put it aside, feeling slightly relieved as he walked away. If only she could have ignored the way his jeans clung to his hips—hadn't that gotten her in trouble with him the first time?

THE HALF-HOUR DRIVE through the Roaring Fork valley was beautiful, the mountains tall sentinels on either side of the highway, their peaks jutting unevenly above the tree line. The women's conversation flowed fast, and Heather was relieved to simply catch up in person rather than over the phone. When they were driving down Main Street in Valentine Valley, she let Emily's enthusiasm for her new hometown sweep over her. Beneath a vivid blue sky dotted with cotton-ball clouds, everything was so picturesque, like an old-fashioned postcard. One- and two-story clapboard or brick stores were interspersed with more majestic stone buildings like the Hotel Colorado and the Royal Theater. Emily slowed down to point toward her bakery, Sugar and Spice, with plate glass windows on either side of the door overflowing with mouthwatering displays of her creative genius, cakes and pastries and tarts. Everywhere planters spilled over with summer flowers, and U.S. flags heralded the coming Fourth of July holiday. People strolled arm in arm down the sidewalks, window-shopping or already carrying loaded bags.

"Do you see all those couples in love?" Emily said happily. "We're known for romance around here—and romance needs food. You really should move here, Heather. You've made no secret that you don't like living in the city. And we don't have a full-time caterer."

"So you've said," Heather began, looking over her shoulder at the hotel they'd just passed. "But that place looks like it would have a wonderful restaurant."

"It does, Main Street Steakhouse—and they get their beef from our ranch," she added proudly, before insisting, "But they're very busy—too busy for a lot of catering."

"Our ranch" was the Silver Creek Ranch, which Emily had told her had been in her fiancé's family for well over a hundred years. They'd raised cattle for generations, working together as a family. Even the groom's sister, Brooke, rode alongside her two brothers and shared in every chore.

They turned the corner where Main Street ended at the imposing town hall, with its clock tower jutting into the sky. And then Heather inhaled at the sight of a beautiful, sprawling Victorian mansion, nestled in the foothills of the nearby mountain range. Turrets rose up through three stories of the beautiful old home, and sunburst trim spanned between every porch rail.

"So this is the Sweetheart Inn," Heather breathed, reluctant to leave the car. "It's as beautiful as you said—with another great restaurant that caters, I bet. And your grandmother owns it?"

Emily nodded as she pulled the keys from the ignition and tossed them in her purse. "My dad mostly works their ranch, but several of my family help out around here. And the restaurant would be relieved to reduce its catering load. They turn away too many customers as it is."

Heather gave a reluctant smile. "You've done your research."

"You bet I have," Emily shot back, opening her car door.

As Heather walked around to the trunk she couldn't help wondering if Chris would be hanging around the inn. She wasn't going to ask about him, of course. If Emily suspected even a hint of interest, she would be trying to fix them up. *Now* that *would be a laugh*, she thought, seeing some humor in the situation for the first time.

Emily paused with her hand on the closed trunk and spoke in a sober voice. "You know, the Sweets could have rejected me. I was the child of a teenage romance, and my mom had lied to Joe Sweet for years about my true parentage. She never did confess before she died, not even to me."

Heather gently touched Emily's arm. "You don't need to relive this again. Memories can be so painful."

"I know you've heard it all before, but when you meet all of my family, I wanted you to remember how special they are. Dad was gentle and understanding about the crazy news, and so glad to know me. My brothers were open to a relationship, even happy they had another sister to tease—though I was their 'big' sister. I know I complained a lot to you about Steph disliking me, but she's really come around, and things are so much better."

Heather pulled her suitcase out of the trunk. So Chris was a nice guy when life threw the family a curve ball. That didn't change the fact that he'd picked her up in a bar—and that she'd let him, *encouraged* him, even. Emily wouldn't want to know such things about the brother she was just getting to know.

Heather forced a determined smile. "You sound so happy."

Emily bit her lip, as if to withhold a quiver. "I have everything I've ever wanted—and a wonderful man to share my life with. I can't wait for you to meet him to-night!"

Emily slammed the trunk and they began to walk up the path toward the wide front porch.

"I'm sure his pictures don't even do him justice. You sound like the perfect bride," Heather added, feeling a mild pang of envy. She cleared her throat. "You're lucky all your wedding guests can stay right where the reception is."

Emily gave her sidelong grin. "A change of topic from all the mushy stuff. I get it. Most of the guests live right here in town, but I'm sure there'll be a few to keep you company—not that I plan on letting you have a moment to yourself. We have such a packed schedule! But I'll give you a couple hours to relax. Can I pick you up around seven for the party? Don't wear anything fancy—it's a jeans-and-cowboy-boots kind of crowd."

Heather smiled. "Who'd have guessed?"

Checking in was painless, and she was able to meet Mrs. Sweet, Emily's very proper grandmother. Her room had an incredible view of the mountains, and for a while she busied herself unpacking. To her surprise, she ended up dozing with her e-reader in her lap, then had to rush to get dressed. She debated over what to wear—everything was too proper or too relaxed. But when she and Emily met up in the lobby, and both were wearing short jean skirts, they burst out laughing and slung their arms around each other. It was as if they'd never been apart.

After a short drive across the little town and closer to the highway, Heather saw that the party was at a dive of a place where the blinking neon sign read TONY'S TAVERN.

Emily laughed at Heather's skeptical look. "This is where Nate and I first met. It holds a special place in my heart, and the owner is a wonderful man, one of Nate's good friends. All the guys hang out here pretty regularly."

The tavern had more neon signs between mounted animal heads and flat screen TVs. As they walked past the bar running along their right, Emily grinned and acknowledged all the well-wishes from jean-clad guys and girls wearing t-shirts and ball caps or cowboy hats.

When they entered a back room furnished with a pool table amidst scattered tables and chairs, there was a burst of cheering that made Emily put a hand to her chest and blink rapidly. "Oh my!"

People rushed forward, and Heather found herself overwhelmed by faces and names. She told herself she'd focus on learning the bridal party's names as soon as she could. At last she met Emily's groom, Nate Thalberg, a tall cowboy with dark wavy hair, and green eyes that barely saw anything beyond Emily. His tender gaze gave Heather all the proof she needed to know that her friend was in good and loving hands.

The bridal couple was swept away in the crowd, and for a moment, she was alone. She eyed a table filled with appetizers, nachos, veggies, and cheese trays, but her stomach was too clenched to eat. Someone put a beer in her hand and she took a cautious sip, knowing she had to stay coldly sober that night. She stiffened as she saw Emily say something to her brother Chris, and then his gaze darted Heather's way.

Oh God.

Alone, he purposefully came toward her, and it was all too much, the worry and the anxiety that had been building up since the moment she'd seen him again. She held up both hands until he came to a stop, then whispered urgently, "Look, you don't need to keep an eye on me. We don't owe each other anything. Nothing's going to happen between us, so let's just pretend—"

"I'm sorry," he interrupted, his stare full of confusion, "but I don't understand what's going on. I've never met you before today at the airport, have I?"

Heather could only gape at him. She'd been nervous all afternoon over how this first meeting alone would go—and he didn't even *remember* her?

Chapter Two

CHRIS SWEET WAS still surprised at how quickly instantaneous anger and lust had come rushing back the moment he'd seen Heather in the airport. *Heather Armstrong.* At least now he knew her full name. She still wore her red hair short and wavy, drawing attention to her wide emerald eyes and high cheekbones. She had womanly curves without the lean look of someone who exercised too much. He'd remembered her immediately, all right, but wouldn't give her the satisfaction of recognition after she'd ditched him in the airport hotel seven months ago without even a good-bye, leaving him no way to track her down.

And he'd humiliated himself by trying for far too long, but no one had remembered seeing the gorgeous redhead but him. Anyone in authority wasn't giving out private information. He'd surely seemed like a desperate stalker to them. It was as if Heather had been some kind of erotic dream—

Until he'd seen her at the Aspen airport that afternoon and been blown away. But he could hardly do anything about it in front of his sister Emily. He'd been as polite as a stranger—and so had Heather. He hadn't been sure what she was thinking, but now he knew. She was wishing they'd never been together, wanted to pretend it had never happened. Well, he'd granted her wish.

Now she was staring at him with wide vulnerable eyes, and for just a moment, he was sympathetic. It probably hurt to be forgotten. And then he remembered she was the type of woman to run out of a hotel room, the type who thought she could dictate how this wedding weekend would go. She'd probably had other men since they'd been together; maybe it was how she got her thrills.

Whereas he hadn't been able to find another woman who intrigued him like she did, and hadn't dated these last seven months. No one had been able to compare to the mysterious, elusive Heather. His family, friends, and single women had certainly noticed that he'd backed off dating, and the busybodies of Valentine Valley were in their glory, spreading rumors that he must have it bad for someone. But he wasn't going to spill his private business—and then someone had taken the decision out of his hands.

Heather blinked at him, as if arousing from a stupor, then spoke stiffly. "Oh. Maybe . . . maybe I was wrong. I thought you were someone else. Sorry."

She actually turned away, and when he imagined some other guy hitting on her—maybe one of his brothers!—he found himself touching her arm. "Where do you think you know me from?"

When she stiffened, he let her go. She didn't quite meet his eyes as she took a sip of the beer. He remembered the way he'd watched her sip drinks at the hotel bar, the sweet curve of her upper lip enticing him with a drop of moisture. He hadn't been able to stop looking at her mouth, and obviously that hadn't changed. He was an idiot.

But she didn't seem to have an answer for him.

"Have you been to Valentine Valley before?" he prodded.

She shook her head, and words seemed dragged out of her. "Emily raved about it, and I was looking forward to checking it out, but . . ." Her words faded, and she shot him a glance that quickly skittered away.

But *he* was here. She might as well have shouted that aloud. He was surprised that he didn't just stalk away from her. But somehow . . . he couldn't. He was getting all mixed up by memories of her rising above him in bed, her eager curiosity, as if she'd never dared be so bold as to sleep with a stranger. All an act, he'd told himself for months afterward.

But now he was staring at her again, torn between anger and the desire that he'd never felt for another woman, and had thought perhaps he'd never feel again. Hell, it made him angry at *himself.*

"So how do you know Emily?" he asked, trying to sound casual.

He was just punishing himself.

A ghost of a smile relaxed those memorable lips. "We met in San Francisco. I was a sous chef at a restaurant she and her ex-husband frequented. She had so much to say about the food, and soon we were meeting for lunch. She was my biggest supporter when I opened my own catering business. Whenever work got too crazy, she did some baking for me." She choked off her words, as if she hadn't meant to speak so freely.

"Oh, that's right, you're one of the reasons she became a pastry chef."

Heather actually blushed, which you couldn't miss on her pale redhead complexion. "She's always been gifted in the kitchen."

He told himself she couldn't be a complete witch, if she was that close to Emily. Women could still be friends and disapprove of each other's sex lives. He'd known she'd been a chef—they hadn't hidden that sort of thing from each other when they'd lounged in bed and talked.

She seemed to be uncomfortable with his silence, saying, "So you're a cowboy."

"Hat and boots give me away?" he shot back, keeping his smile fixed and pleasant. He leaned closer. "Or maybe it's the smell."

She backed away so quickly he almost laughed.

"Sorry. Ranch joke."

There was a moment of awkward silence, and he should have walked away.

"Emily says you work with your family," she said.

He nodded, surprised that she sounded curious. That had to be faked. If she was really curious about him, she wouldn't have run out when he'd gone for coffee. "Yeah, I have two brothers and two sisters, including Emily." He pointed to Will and Daniel playing a competitive game of pool. "People say that my brothers and I look alike."

"It's the blond hair," she murmured, frowning. "And the smell."

It was his turn to blink at her. Why had she bothered to continue with the joke?

She shook her head. "Sorry. I—I must be keeping you from your family, from the groom. It's Emily and Nate's big weekend, after all."

For a moment, he could have sworn he caught a glimpse of bleakness in her eyes. Naw. And then the truth almost spilled from him, his anger and betrayal. He had to escape before he made a mistake. "Yeah, you're right. See you around."

And then to put her in her place, he asked Monica Shaw to dance. Monica was sleek, elegant, and model-thin, with caramel skin and dark curls that danced to her shoulders. One of Emily's other bridesmaids, she owned Monica's Flowers and Gifts on Main Street.

Monica gave him a teasing frown. "Why, Chris Sweet, are you taking pity on one of the only women here without a man?"

"As if you need a man," he shot back.

She grinned and let him swing her out onto the dance floor. He tried not to look at Heather, who was still standing alone, but once or twice caught himself doing just that.

"So who's the redhead?" Monica asked.

Chris strove for nonchalance. "Heather Armstrong."

Monica craned her neck, making it really obvious she was staring. "Em's friend from Frisco! I was late to the party and missed the introductions." She eyed him with speculation. "I saw you talking to her. You looked quite cozy. She shoot you down?"

He hesitated. "Something like that."

"That doesn't happen to you too often, does it? At least it didn't use to, but lately you've been a lonely guy." She patted his shoulder. "Don't take it too personally. It's a busy weekend when you're a member of the wedding party. But then you'll find that out."

"You have experience?"

After an exaggerated sigh, she said, "One too many times! Always the bridesmaid, you know. But don't tell Emily I said that," she added with a bright smile.

Suddenly the music stopped and Josh Thalberg raised his arms for quiet.

"Welcome to our bachelor/bachelorette party," he said, followed by thunderous applause and cheering. Josh was the groom's brother, another cowboy, but with a talent for leather carving that made his work in demand, even in Aspen, Chris had heard.

Chris glanced toward Heather, and found himself feeling relieved when he saw that she was standing beside Nate's sister, Brooke. At least he wouldn't have to feel like it was his responsibility to keep her occupied. Brooke worked the family ranch alongside her brothers, and Chris had never been surprised that she did the job as well as any cowboy he knew. The two of them always had good discussions about the books they'd read. Now she was with Chris's old high-school football teammate, Adam Desantis, an ex-Marine who'd had a rocky road settling back into Valentine.

Chris felt uneasy that he didn't like the thought of Heather feeling alone and on the outside. He didn't have to care about her—she made it clear she didn't want that from him.

"It's a Jack and Jill party!" Brooke called almost gleefully.

Josh gave his sister a mock frown. "I'm the best man, and I voted that silly name down."

Brooke elbowed Heather and laughed. Heather smiled, but there wasn't much merriment in it. She stole a glance at Chris and quickly looked away. Why was she so uneasy? After the way she'd left him behind, why should she care that he might not remember her? He thought he'd gotten a small score for himself, but now he had to wonder . . .

"We had a few games in mind," Josh continued, smiling as the bride and groom exchanged glances and rolled their eyes. "One I thought could prove a lot of fun. We'd blindfold Emily and make her guess by touch which butt is Nate's."

"You can forget that!" Emily called sweetly. After some good-natured male disappointment, she folded her arms across her chest. "As if I'm giving any of you a thrill tonight."

"That's reserved for me," Nate added.

"Not tonight it isn't," she reminded him. "You'll be sleeping at the ranch until we're married."

Chris found himself grinning along with the rest, watching Nate's exaggerated dismay.

"So since we won't subject Emily to the butt game," Josh continued, "we came up with a Scavenger Hunt."

"We?" Brooke echoed. "You mean the internet came up with that."

He grinned at her. "Whatever. When your team gets the list and the game is started, you find the items or place and take a picture. Heck, there'll be points for creativity, too, so put yourselves in the photo. And no cars. We're all walking tonight, people, even though the sun has just about set."

Some of the women groaned, but he ignored them.

"Everyone can pick teams of two or three except the wedding party. We get to hunt along with our future partners from the wedding aisle."

Chris once again found himself glancing at Heather, and Monica smirked at him. He'd never been very good at hiding his emotions. Heather looked back at him with wariness and even resignation.

"And since we have an extra usher—Brooke must have forced Nate to include her boyfriend—"

"Hey!" Brooke called above the chuckles of the crowd. "I did not!"

"I think we can let our new friend, Heather Armstrong, be a team with two of the Sweet brothers, Chris and Will."

Heather's complexion paled even further, although she smiled for everyone's benefit.

Chris almost wanted to voice his own protest—could

they at least have Daniel, who was far more relaxed and easygoing? Will would most likely hit on Heather, and Chris didn't want to see that.

But, of course, Heather was free to do what she wanted. And she'd made it clear she didn't want Chris.

She gave Will a game smile, especially when he strode across the room, tall and muscled, a cleft in his chin, a daredevil look peeking out from beneath a lock of sandy hair.

Great, just great, Chris thought.

Chapter Three

HEATHER HAD KNOWN deep in her bones she'd end up on a team with Chris, who'd thought her so unimportant that he'd thrown out her phone number back at the hotel and promptly forgot what she even looked like. So she was relieved when Will Sweet would also be joining them.

She sized up Will in an instant as he walked across the room, all swagger and cockiness. He knew how to make a girl feel important with the directness of his gaze, but he came across as amusing rather than threatening, and she appreciated that. All around them, other people gathered together in groups, and Brooke passed out the scavenger hunt clues.

The conversations about scavenger hunt strategy were so loud, Will had to raise his voice as he held out a hand. "Will Sweet. Good to meet you, Heather."

His grip was firm, his manner attentive, and intense hazel eyes made her feel like the only woman in the room—but she didn't fall for that stuff easily, never had. Will was obviously the kind of guy who made *every* woman feel special.

"So, Heather," Will said, as Chris approached, "I hear you're from San Francisco."

"She's the caterer who got Em interested in baking," Chris offered.

She almost said she could speak for herself, but didn't want her anger and disappointment to turn her into a bitch.

"So it must be strange to be in our little village," Will continued, "you being a city girl and all."

"Actually, I grew up in a small California mountain town," she said. "I'm not all that fond of San Francisco. Too big and hectic and crowded."

Chris looked surprised at her revelation, and she didn't know why—after all, she was just a stranger to him.

"But your business is there," Chris said.

She shrugged. "I've been thinking of relocating."

"Then you need to come to Valentine," Will said, lifting his beer as if in a toast.

Just what she'd been considering—until she'd learned that Chris lived here. Other people had brief affairs and moved past them; for her, it had been difficult to forget, these last seven months. But seeing Chris on a regular basis? How would she handle that?

"I don't know," she hedged. "I have a brother with a couple kids back in California. Not sure I want to be so far away."

"Then we won't push her, right, Will?" Chris said pointedly to his brother.

She felt a twinge of hurt until she remembered that he had no reason to want her gone—he didn't remember her. She could have groaned. How long would it take to get over this feeling of insignificance? She'd done the wildest, bravest thing of her life with Chris Sweet, and it hadn't even registered with him.

Chris and Will eyed each other, and although she couldn't read their expressions, she thought that perhaps Will had picked up on something. She grew tense, but he didn't say anything, simply took the scavenger list that Brooke offered to Heather.

Brooke gave Heather a sympathetic smile. "Good luck with these guys. You'll need it."

Heather inwardly winced. Will scanned the list, even as his smile widened.

"Let the rest of us see," Chris reminded him.

Will held up the list in front of him, as if he wasn't about to relinquish his self-prescribed leadership position. Heather and Chris ended up shoulder to shoulder, and it was hard to for her to even read, as she tried to fight off her reaction to his nearness. It had been just this way as they sat side-by-side at the bar that snowy night, few people around them, talking so intently that they leaned closer and closer to hear each other over the music. Hands had met, shoulders brushed—and she'd felt more wired and alive than ever before.

Sadly, he still seemed to have that affect on her. She had to swallow for moisture, and the touch of his arm felt warm and hard and male. Though Will still smiled, he watched them closely, so she forced herself to read—and soon knew why Chris gave an amused groan.

"This is interesting," Chris said.

"Interesting?" Heather echoed in disbelief. "We really have to bring back a banana and a donut?"

Will chuckled. "Raunchy, but it *is* a bachelor/bachelorette party."

"Can't we just do a pencil rubbing at a cemetery? You know, the traditional stuff?"

"That's on there, too," Chris pointed out. "But it has to be the oldest grave in the cemetery, so you're lucky you have us. We know the cemetery."

"You mean *you* know it," Will said. "I didn't exactly spend time there."

Chris glanced at Heather with that smile that had once given her goose bumps.

"When we were kids, our mom liked to walk through the cemetery, picking pine cones and reading the tombstones. She made pinecone wreaths for Christmas gifts. Will got out of it when he could, but I didn't mind going with her."

It was hard to hate him, she thought with a sigh.

When everyone had a list and a few moments to strategize, Josh said, "Once you leave here, you have an hour and a half to get as many pictures as you can. Good luck, and . . . start!"

Heather would have remained at the back of the pack, but she thought Will would pick her up and drag her along, by the impatient yet genial way he bumped shoulders with opponents to get a good start.

She found herself rolling her eyes.

Chris chuckled. "Sorry, my brother is competitive."

"Not you?" she asked, as they emerged into the twilight.

He hesitated, and his expression briefly altered. "I can be," was his only response.

"You're probably competitive over women, like most guys," she said.

He eyed her with interest, and she regretted prying. But again—it wouldn't mean anything to him.

"I haven't known many women to feel competitive about."

She didn't believe him. He must have had a lot of women, to so easily forget their days together.

Will slung an arm around Chris's neck, as if he were about to childishly rub his knuckles into his scalp, but instead just pulled him off-stride. "My brother used to do his fair share of dating, but not lately."

Chris eluded the maneuver with long-practiced ease. "I just happen to be pickier than you."

Heather flinched a bit, knowing she was taking everything he said in a way he didn't mean.

Will picked up his pace, then looked back at Heather's feet pointedly. "At least your sandals don't have really high heels. Can you hurry up, or will I need to put you on my back?"

"Ignore him," Chris said. "It's just a game."

But Heather could be as competitive as anyone else, and as she picked up her speed, found herself suggesting the strategy of going to the cemetery first, before it got too dark. The Sweet brothers liked that idea—as well as the fact that the cemetery might be the farthest away they'd have to go. They ducked between the apartment complex buildings to hide their intention.

Heather finally relaxed over the next hour and a half. The Sweet brothers were a lot of fun, and she was successful in putting her past with Chris briefly out of her mind. Will wanted to take the photos creatively, so they ended up acting out the "Twilight" book trilogy, with Will as the vampire, Chris as the werewolf, and she as "Bella," the girl torn between them. She didn't like the "romantic triangle" idea so much—it had been Will's inspiration, since their sister Steph had been a fan. But acting out being bitten by a vampire on top of the stone bridge in the Rose Garden was actually kind of fun. Chris, the werewolf, stalked her in the cemetery as she hid near the oldest tombstone.

The scavenger hunt turned more difficult when they had to photograph a metaphor for the bride and the groom. It was easy to find an "Ask Me Why I'm Sugar and Spice" apron from Emily's bakery, although they made it funny by having Will wear it in the picture. But cowboy stuff was harder to appropriate when they couldn't hike out to the nearest ranch and most stores were closed. Chris suggested propping a cowboy hat on a computer monitor, to represent both aspects of Nate's partly administrative duties at the Silver Creek Ranch. They ducked into the Hotel Colorado, where Chris knew the manager, to borrow a computer and desk. After setting up the hat and computer, Heather dramatically collapsed across the desk, red lipstick trailing down her neck.

For the next clue, "Find three people who will write a sentence about why the groom/bride should dump the other and marry them," they ended up at the True Grits Diner, where several of the customers eagerly volunteered, as long as they could play werewolf or vampire victims in the photo. "Edward" and "Jacob" were pretty bloodthirsty in this scavenger drama.

They had to run the several blocks back to Tony's to beat the deadline, then took the "Where Emily and Nate met" photo in the front of the bar, where "Bella" made it clear in the photo that she chose "Edward" over "Jacob."

In the back room, all the party guests were downing appetizers as if they hadn't seen food in days, talking and laughing over the results of the game. They all attached their photos to Josh by e-mail, and he displayed them on a screen, connecting his laptop to a projector. Heather felt embarrassed and silly when their photos got the most guffaws and applause, but the judges, Nate and Emily, declared them the winners. There were calls for some reenactments, but she pled her way out of that. It felt different to be fought over by the Sweet brothers where everyone could watch and comment. She wasn't used to being so on display, and she noticed that Chris took a backseat just like she did, letting Will do all the boasting, bragging, and celebrating.

The cake Nate had baked just for Emily was cut, and she brought Heather a slice.

"Congratulations," Emily said. "I have to admit, I

was worried you wouldn't enjoy a scavenger hunt with strangers."

Heather waved a hand in easy dismissal of Emily's concerns, then eyed the chocolate cake with greedy interest. "Did he use one of your recipes?"

"I don't know, but you're avoiding my pointed comment."

Heather took a forkful and chewed, letting the taste coat her tongue. "Not bad."

"Heather!"

She shrugged. "What was I supposed to do, back out?"

"Frankly, once you might have. You can be pretty shy."

Heather realized that meeting Chris seven months ago had changed her in more ways than one. She'd done something truly daring, taken a risk. Although it was hurting her now, she couldn't regret what she'd done. It made her a little braver.

Was that also the reason she was considering leaving San Francisco, when it would be so easy to stay where her business was thriving?

"And being partnered with my brothers," Emily continued, eyeing her a little too closely, "well, they're two very different people. Looks like you handled them okay."

"They didn't need to be handled," Heather insisted. "I was the one who was embarrassed and reluctant. They put me at ease."

"And put you at the center of their little drama. They can be pretty competitive with each other."

"No worries here. I'm not about to be anyone's prize this weekend. I'm just going to be a great bridesmaid."

Emily's smile softened. "And a great friend. I'm so glad you came!"

They hugged before Emily moved on to fulfill her bridely duty of socializing. Heather watched a wild game of beer pong for a while, but she didn't join in, conscious of her need to stay sober. She surreptitiously kept an eye on Chris, who'd decided to play pool. It was as if she were on pins and needles, waiting for him to have a sudden memory of her and reveal everything.

Yet she was torn in so many directions, because a part of her still ached that he'd forgotten what she'd considered magical, and another part of her was angry. She was frankly glad when the evening began to wind down and she could soon go back to the inn and collapse in her room.

Emily returned to her. "If you don't mind, Chris is going to give you a ride back to the inn. It's on his way, and we still have some cleanup here."

Heather hastily said, "Then let me stay and help. That's what a bridesmaid does."

"Not a bridesmaid who traveled all day today. You look exhausted—and then you had to run around town for a silly game. Go home and rest. My sister Steph will pick you up at 10:30 tomorrow morning for the bridal brunch at the Widows' Boardinghouse."

Heather gave a tired smile. "I am certainly looking forward to that. I've heard so much about those old ladies. I'm surprised they didn't attend tonight."

"There was some concern that they'd crash the party," Emily admitted, "only because they've hinted at a sur-

prise in store for us, but I guess I'll just have to keep waiting and wondering. Now go to the inn and rest. I have
plenty of help."

Heather saw Chris at the door to the main bar, shrugging into a light jacket. He gave her a smile and motioned
with his head, and sighing, she approached him.

"You didn't have to offer, Chris," Heather quietly said.
"You already went out of your way for me today."

"Trust me, you're on my way. Now come on, my pickup's out front."

CHRIS STARTED THE pickup, feeling the same sense of
unease that hadn't gone away all night. Heather was quiet
beside him, her face turned slightly toward the window.
By the dashboard lights, he could see her profile, the
straight nose, the curve of her cheek, the downcast eyes.

And he felt terrible for lying to her.

Then his emotions swayed the other way, back to his
anger that she'd left him so abruptly.

Yet . . . tonight he'd seen other sides of her nature, fun-
loving, creative, adventurous. She hadn't once responded
to Will's open flirtation with anything other than cheer-
ful amusement. She'd been respectful in the cemetery,
persuasive with the customers at the diner to get them to
go along with the prank—and damn hot, as she'd acted
as the vampire victim. She did manage to avoid being his
werewolf victim, and he understood why.

And he was drawn to her all over again. He had to get
past this, and lies weren't going to help.

When he pulled up to the Sweetheart Inn a few minutes later, she gave him a smile and removed her seatbelt. "Thanks, Chris. I'll see you tomorrow night at the wedding rehearsal."

"Heather, wait. Can we talk?"

Eyes narrowed with suspicion, she kept her hand on the door handle. "About what?"

He sighed. "Look, this is awkward to say, and I regret I ever started it, but . . . I remember you. I remember everything."

Chapter Four

THE SHOCK MADE Heather grip the door handle so hard that her fingernails almost cut into her palms.

She shot him a suspicious glance, afraid to assume what he meant. "What are you saying? Exactly what do you remember?"

"Our two nights in the Denver airport hotel."

She took a deep breath, anger and humiliation sweeping over her like a wave of heat. "You're saying you recognized me the moment we saw each other again?"

He nodded.

"And you thought it okay to *lie* about it, to pretend we'd never met—to *hurt* me? Why would you do that?"

"Because you hurt me," he said impassively.

She gaped at him in disbelief. At least he didn't look away from her like a coward.

"I hurt *you*?" she cried. "I left you my phone number

in a note and you never called! You don't think that was a slap in the face?"

"What?" he said with astonishment.

He leaned toward her, and she pressed herself against the door, trying hard not to cry.

"You never left me your phone number," he insisted.

"I did! You were out getting coffee when I got the call from the airline. I had to get there immediately to make the only plane to the coast, so I left the note right on the bureau. I kept waiting for your call and it never came." Her voice dropped into a hoarse whisper as she revealed how much he'd meant to her.

He was staring hard at her now, and then he sighed. "I never got it, Heather. I don't know if a draft slid it behind the bureau or what, but when I came back, you were gone. When you didn't return, I was furious."

She met his stare with her own, her mind all jumbled and trying to rearrange itself. "You—you really never got it? I felt so . . . sleazy, thinking I had misread everything."

"Sleazy? God, I never wanted you to feel that," he insisted. He ran a hand through his hair and gave a faint smile. "I made a fool of myself trying to find you. I even called restaurants in San Francisco until I thought someone would call the police on me."

She sagged back against her door, unable to stop staring at him. "You . . . tried to find me?"

He nodded, and suddenly the tension in the pickup seemed to shift, all the astonishment morphing into something else, something yearning and sexual, primitive and dark. She couldn't seem to take a deep breath.

"I—I don't know what to say," she whispered shakily. "I've been thinking such bad things about you—and bad things about myself."

"I never wanted that," he said quietly, reaching for her hand.

She pulled away, afraid if he touched her, she'd lose all rational thought, just as he'd done to her that snowy night. He'd held her hand at the bar, and they'd leaned in to kiss, and she hadn't cared what they looked like to outsiders.

If he was hurt by the distance she put between them now, he didn't show it.

"Don't ever think badly about yourself, Heather. I've never felt like I did with you, and haven't felt like that since."

"Me neither," she whispered, wishing she could tear her gaze away from his face, the lean line of his jaw, the hungry way his eyes watched her. She put up a hand. "But this has to stop."

"What has to stop?" he asked hoarsely. "A conversation?"

She waved her hand. "This. Whatever *this* is starting to feel like. I don't want people to know about what we did, Chris."

"Of course not. It's no one's business but ours."

"If we keep looking at each other like this, Emily will start to suspect, and I just couldn't live that down. I'd never done anything like that, and haven't since. I think I sort of scared myself."

"I can't say I scared myself," he said dryly, "but I've

never done anything like that either. No one ever made me want to—until you."

Her lips parted, her mouth was dry, and suddenly she thought the only way to recover was to kiss him until they were both senseless.

Oh, this was *not* good.

She took a deep breath. "Chris, we need to take a step back."

He frowned. "I can't do that."

"You have to! At least for the weekend. After that—I don't know. If Emily found out right now, during her wedding weekend when she has enough to worry about—I'd be so embarrassed, and it might affect our friendship. I won't risk losing her."

"You sound like you think I'd tell her." His brows lowered in a frown.

"I know you wouldn't mean to, but it might come out. I can't take that chance. I don't know you at all, Chris."

"I think you do. We only had two days, but you *know* me."

"I—I'm sorry."

He turned away from her and gripped the steering wheel. "I won't hang all over you, but we're going to talk more about this. And that's a promise."

Biting her lip, she got out of the pickup and shut the door. She waited for Chris to accelerate hard to get away from her, but he didn't move until she was opening the big front door of the inn. After he'd pulled away, she shut it without going inside, and went to sit on the porch instead, finding a big wicker chair to sink into. Then she clasped her knees to her chest, buried her face, and just tried to breathe the cool evening air.

Everything was different—*she* was different. And she didn't know what to do about it.

HEATHER HAD PUT herself together—sort of—by mid-morning. To her surprise, she'd actually slept well and deeply. She no longer harbored anger toward Chris—and she couldn't blame him for not telling the truth immediately, since he'd believed the worst of her as she had of him—but she didn't know what emotions she was left with besides desire. And she wasn't about to linger on that in the middle of Emily's wedding.

She was sitting on the porch once again, near hanging baskets of red and white impatiens, when a battered pickup pulled up the circular drive. At first she tensed, thinking it was Chris, but then she saw a blond girl wave at her through the windows.

Steph Sweet, Emily and Chris's younger sister, she thought with relief. Heather had been introduced to her at Tony's Tavern last night, but they hadn't had a chance to talk. Steph was a blonder, prettier version of her brothers, heading toward her senior year in high school. During the ride, she peppered Heather with questions about Emily in San Francisco, talked about her own waitressing and barrel-racing, and barely let Heather get a word in. It was actually a relief.

The Widows' Boardinghouse was just outside of town, down a gravel road along the Silver Creek, and part of the Silver Creek Ranch itself. It was an old Victorian with wrap-around porches and gingerbread trim, and there was even a professional sign with WIDOWS' BOARD-INGHOUSE in block letters. That made her laugh.

Steph shook her head as she grinned. "These old ladies sure are something."

"How many live here again?"

"Just three—Mrs. Thalberg, the groom's grandma; Mrs. Palmer, Brooke's future grandma-in-law—if Adam ever asks her to marry him; and Mrs. Ludlow, who's the sanest one of the bunch, the only one who really behaves like you'd think a grandma would. They all work part-time for Emily at the bakery."

Heather smiled and opened the car door. "I hear they're very interested in everybody's business in Valentine Valley."

"That depends on how you view it." Steph came around the front of the pickup. "They're the main force behind the Valentine Valley Preservation Fund. They're a big help when a person wants to open a new business or renovate an old building. But there are some people—like my Grandma Sweet—who think they can be busybodies."

"Well, I'm really looking forward to meeting them."

The bridal brunch took place on the back porch, where linen cloths covered picnic tables, and huge pitch-ers of lemonade and iced tea were available to quench a summer's thirst. Heather hugged Emily, and renewed her brief acquaintance with Monica Shaw and Brooke Thal-berg, the other bridesmaids. Steph, as the maid of honor, seemed to take pleasure in the official duty of introducing

Heather to the three elderly women. Mrs. Thalberg was dressed in capris, a blouse, and a jean vest, her hair dyed a brilliant red, her makeup artfully disguising her age. Mrs. Palmer, with a bright blond wig perched atop her head, wore an outrageous dress with sunflowers all over it and spoke with a Western twang. Mrs. Ludlow was just as Steph had said, a conservatively dressed white-haired old lady leaning over a walker, but whose bright, intelligent eyes missed nothing.

Nate's mom and Emily's stepmom had their heads together in a corner, talking wedding details, Heather assumed, as she was introduced. Sandy Thalberg, who had MS and leaned on a cane, had dark hair framing a lively face, and looked completely different from Faith Sweet, with her flowing skirt and blouse, jingling bracelets on each wrist, and loose, frizzy hair shot with gray.

Over lunch, Heather enjoyed the flow of feminine conversation, and did her best to try to see how all these women fit into Emily's life. Heather was the only outsider, and she felt a yearning to be a part of their circle, a part of the bond of family and friendship that's often synonymous with small-town living. Her own parents were dead, and her brother lived just far enough away in southern California to make visits only a few times a year rather than a few times a month.

After helping to take the leftovers into the cow-themed kitchen, all the women waited in the living room, or "the parlor," as Mrs. Palmer drawled, for the bride to try on her wedding gown for the last fitting. Mrs. Thalberg told Heather about the widows finding Emily's grandmother's wedding dress in the attic, and how Mrs. Ludlow had done the alterations for the excited bride.

And when at last Emily came floating down the staircase in white satin, with airy lace at the top of the bodice and all the way down long, narrow sleeves, every woman sighed with pleasure and awe.

"That dress is just like Grace Kelly's," Mrs. Thalberg said, clearing her throat. "The first time I saw it, I knew Emily would look beautiful in it."

"I'm so excited for the weddin'," Mrs. Palmer said. "We have a special surprise in store for our dear Emily and Nate."

Emily, who was looking down at herself wearing a dreamy smile, glanced up. "A surprise?"

Brooke and Monica exchanged uneasy glances.

Brooke said to Mrs. Thalberg, "Grandma, now you know Emily has the schedule for ceremony down pat. You can't add anything to it at this late date."

"Oh, it's not for the wedding," Mrs. Thalberg insisted. "It's for the reception. Plenty of time there."

"You didn't tell us about this," the mother of the groom said to her mother-in-law in a curious voice.

From her seat on a stool near Emily's voluminous skirts, Mrs. Ludlow spoke around pins in her mouth. "Then it wouldn't be a surprise, now would it?"

Shaking her head, Emily only laughed and looked with fondness from one widow to the next. "I can't wait," she said earnestly. "Although please, don't go to too much trouble."

"No trouble at all," Mrs. Thalberg said with satisfaction. "After all, you're about to be my new granddaughter, so that needs a special welcome."

Emily reached out to take Mrs. Thalberg's hand. "You've been nothing but wonderful since the moment I arrived here without money or a place to stay."

They stared into each other's eyes, and suddenly the mood of the onlookers changed from uneasy curiosity to tenderness. Emily had told Heather that the widows had been good friends of her Grandma Riley, the first to wear the beautiful dress. And now that dress was a connection between generations.

Heather felt the lump in her throat and questioned its source. She was so happy for the new life Emily had found, but did that make her yearn for her own fulfillment?

While Emily changed, Heather began to help box the glass vases for the floating candle centerpieces.

"So what do you think of my brother?" Steph suddenly asked as she wrapped a vase.

Heather tried not to stiffen. "Huh?"

"Sorry, should have said 'brothers.' I liked your photos from the scavenger hunt."

"Oh, yeah," Heather said, averting her flushed face. "Your brothers were nice, especially getting stuck with the new girl in town."

"Trust me, they didn't mind that."

Heather hesitated, then found ill-advised words tumbling out. "None of your brothers brought dates last night. That surprised me."

She shrugged. "There's always women hanging on Will. I think he thought he'd have a better time at a bachelor/

bachelorette party without arm candy. Daniel—he just graduated from college last month, so no new girlfriends for him yet. As for Chris, I don't know, he seems focused on the ranch lately. I don't remember the last time he had a date."

Heather took a deep breath. *Could he really have been as affected by her as she was by him?*

"He had a steady girl in college, but that fell apart when she moved to Denver after graduation. He wasn't about to do that. He's not too fond of the big city."

To Heather's dismay, she saw Emily watching them thoughtfully.

"I totally understand about city life," Heather said to Steph. "I'm not too fond of it myself. What about you? Don't some of your friends long to move away?"

But the teenager, pulling out a long piece of packing tape, her gaze unfocused, didn't seem to hear her. "I sometimes worry it was my fault Chris didn't move to Denver."

Heather frowned. "That can't be true. He's a cowboy—what would he do in Denver? And it seems to me your family is devoted to your ranch."

Steph shrugged. "I was in middle school when he graduated, and I used to call him all the time, whining about my braces, or the boy I had a crush on, or another fight with Daniel. I poured my heart out to him, so I sort of wonder—did he feel I needed him too much?"

"It sounds like he's a good brother, but I don't think he'd make a major life decision because you needed a shoulder. Yet I'm certain he's happy to be here for you," she added quickly.

Steph grinned. "Thanks. It's nice to have a second opinion. My brothers are good guys. They're keeping Nate company today."

"Good for them," Heather murmured, pretending she was having a hard time finding another box.

"They're having lunch right now at the Sweetheart Inn, and then hanging out at the hot springs."

Heather straightened. "Hot springs?"

"Oh right, you're staying there. It's right behind the inn. There's a path up into the foothills. You can't miss it."

Heather didn't look at Emily, certain her friend was still studying her. Heather was only curious about the hot springs, and not because the guys were there. Really, she told herself.

Because she certainly wasn't going to chase after Chris Sweet. Not when she'd already said they would have to stay away from each other.

Chapter Five

STEPH DROPPED HEATHER off at the Sweetheart Inn,
and when she should have gone right to her room, she
found herself pausing in the lobby, her mind whirling.
She barely noticed the old-fashioned "parlor" feel, the ma-
hogany furniture, the stained glass lamps scattered about.

Why couldn't she get out of her mind that Chris had
stopped dating after meeting her? What did it matter?

Then she saw the huge family portrait, and she paused
in front of it. Several generations of Sweets had gathered
against a backdrop of shrubs and trees, and it was easy
for Heather to find Chris. He'd been in his early twenties when it was taken, blue eyes sparkling, looking as if
he anticipated his whole future—and liked it. She didn't
know what to think about him, except that she was still
so attracted to him.

And then she was striding across the lobby toward
the door to the stone terrace, where guests ate outside be-

neath several overhead trellises. A pool and hot tub were a refreshing retreat on a June day, but she passed them by, looking for the path that wound along the stream. There was even a little sign shaped like an arrow that said HOT SPRINGS for her to follow.

She walked in silence for several hundred yards, until the clatter of silverware against dishes from the luncheon guests receded, and birdsong mixed with the gurgling of the stream washing down from the mountains. The path twisted through the aspen and evergreen trees, gradually sloping up into the foothills, and soon she heard the deep voices of men.

What the heck had she intended to do? Jump out and yell "Surprise"?

And then she realized she could just see them through the trees, and squatted down, afraid they'd think she was spying on them. She *was* spying. She should turn and run until she was far, far away.

Why did Chris Sweet bring out the risky behavior she never displayed with anyone else?

For long minutes, the men teased the groom about his supposed obsession with Emily, and how she had him "wrapped around her little finger."

"No more ladies for you, Nate."

That was Will's voice, and she heard the answering chuckles.

"He doesn't need anyone but Emily," Chris said mildly.

"Yeah, leave the ladies for Chris."

Heather stiffened, trying to identify the voice—Josh Thalberg?

"Let's not," Chris said.

"Why not?" Will demanded. "Lately you've been pretending you're this shy guy in Valentine, but we all know once you leave the town limits you start picking up women in airports."

Heather covered her mouth to hide a gasp, ignoring the laughter and teasing of the men. They all *knew*—and he'd done this before? He'd bragged about her! She felt the sickness of being used wash over her again.

She was so distraught, she didn't take enough care not to be seen. The sounds of the men getting out of the hot springs didn't register for a moment, and when she lifted her head, her eyes met Chris's through an opening in the trees. She hunkered down again, ducking behind a tree along the path.

All of the men trooped by, talking and laughing. When she peered out after they passed, she saw them all in shorts, some with wet t-shirts on, towels around their necks or trailing from their hands, but no sign of Chris.

She emerged onto the path, ready to run, but once again, she felt drawn to look for him, and saw him still behind the short stone wall that enveloped the hot springs. He was watching her—his knowing eyes daring her.

She stiffened. She wasn't about to run from him and cry in her pillow. No, it was time for a confrontation. She marched up the path and around the bend. The meandering stream opened up before her, a built-up rock pool alongside it. Steam misted around Chris, who now sat in the hot springs up to his shoulders, arms resting on the uneven ledge.

"Were you coming to join us?" he asked. "Or just coming to eavesdrop?"

"I didn't intend to eavesdrop, although I was curious," she said stiffly. "But now I regret it—or maybe it's been a good thing after all. Because I've caught you in another lie, and I should know that about you."

She saw his jaw clench, but his voice was still mild as he spoke.

"What do you think I lied about?"

"Us! Everything!" She lowered her voice and stepped closer to stand above him, hands on her hips. "You told me you'd never done what—what we did before, and now the whole town knows you pick up women in airports! That's just—that's disgusting!"

"I don't pick up women in airports—at least not anybody before or after you."

"I heard what your brother said! He *knew*!"

Chris sighed. "Do you want to hear the reason, or do you just prefer to assume you know everything?"

She opened her mouth, convinced of the righteousness of her position, then sat down primly on a rustic bench. "Go ahead, try to defend yourself."

"Thank you. And I'm not defending myself, just explaining the truth. I didn't want to tell you this, because I knew you'd feel bad. Though I didn't realize it until later, a friend of a friend recognized me that first night in the bar, saw us flirting—and saw us leave together to get a room."

Her mouth dropped open.

"Don't worry, she didn't get all that good of a look at you."

Right. She put a hand to her stomach, which seemed to be twisting like a snake inside her. Great, now she'd be waiting all weekend for this person to recognize her.

"Gossip spreads, of course, and I took some ribbing from my friends. I didn't bother responding. But when I didn't continue to date, that set people wondering about my 'mystery lady.' Nosy people like to have something to talk about, that's all. But count on my brother to bring it up at the worst possible moment."

She studied him, and he didn't look away.

"I'm sorry, Heather," he said with earnest sincerity. "I knew this would bother you. I didn't think you needed to know, and hoped I could spare you from it."

She took a deep breath and exhaled, her shoulders slumping. "I believe you. And I can only imagine how embarrassed you felt."

He leaned his head back against the rocks, his skin glistening with moisture, and gave her a faint smile. "I'm a guy. It was hardly the worst thing people could think of me." His smile faded as their gazes locked. "I wouldn't change a thing."

Once again, simply looking at him made her forget everything but the memories she still carried—how they'd kissed at the bar, how she found herself waiting in the lobby as he'd registered for a room. The fact that someone had watched them faded into the background of her mind, as her body was overcome by the memories of the two of them alone in the elevator, kissing wildly, passionately, until it stopped on their floor. They'd held hands down the corridor, the walk taking forever. She could still hear the sound of the sliding key card, their frantic breathing, almost feel the way he'd pinned her up against the wall and kissed her like the world was ending and they only had each other.

Maybe he was remembering the same things, because he stared at her, hot blue eyes heavily lidded, even as he slowly rose to a standing position. Water sluiced down his naked chest; the light dusting of hair was darkened with moisture. He put his hands on the rocks along the edge, leaning toward her, the sleek muscles of his arms bunching with tension.

Heather felt lost, awash in sensual memories all mixed up with the present. He was there before her, his goal unmistakable, and all she could do was lean toward him and let their mouths meet. Heat was a flash through her, warming her, making her thighs press together. She was hungry for him, for the way he'd made her feel back in Denver, and how she longed to feel it again. All her promises to herself faded away with each kiss, their parted lips touching and tasting, until their mouths opened so they could have more. They touched in no other way, so all her awareness was in her lips and tongue, merging with his.

And then he lifted his head, his breathing as labored as her own. "I don't suppose you're up for some skinny dipping. I certainly am."

She sat back, then with a groan, she ran a hand down her face. "Oh damn, I didn't mean to kiss you."

"I won't tell anyone."

She attempted a glare, even as he chuckled. But her

glare was half-hearted at best, and at last she smiled. "That's not funny."

"You're smiling. It's the first genuine smile I've seen aimed at me since you arrived. You look beautiful."

His voice dropped away into a huskiness that made her shiver.

She stood up, her legs shaky. "I have to go."

"You sure you don't want to get in here with me? It's mighty nice."

"Don't tempt me. We *both* have to get ready for the rehearsal."

"Tempted, are you? That's a good sign."

Shaking her head, biting her lip to keep from smiling, she walked quickly down the path.

"See you later!" he called.

WHEN HE ARRIVED at the park that ran along Silver Creek at four that afternoon, Chris found himself eagerly awaiting his first sight of Heather. He'd almost called to see if she wanted a ride to the wedding rehearsal, but changed his mind. She wanted him to keep his distance this weekend, and he promised he'd try—for now.

But how difficult would that be after the kiss they'd shared? It brought back every memory of that snowy weekend, her uninhibited response to his touch, her playfulness, her passion. Those memories had taunted him when word had circulated through his own hometown that he'd picked up a woman in an airport—a woman he thought had blown him off, not that anyone knew that detail. Frankly, he'd never confirmed or denied anything, even when his brothers had ridden him hard. The fact that only he and Heather shared those memories made it all the more intimate and sexy.

He parked his car near the picnic grove and headed toward the gazebo that overlooked the creek. It was a large, round structure, all painted white, with a railing that circled it, and two stairways leading up, front and back. Flowers and bushes enhanced it, winding among many benches. He figured by tomorrow, Monica's Flowers and Gifts would have it decorated to the hilt, but tonight, its only decoration were the women who gathered inside, talking animatedly, the bride and her court. Emily carried a strange bouquet made out of a paper plate and dozens of multi-colored ribbons that fluttered around her skirt like butterflies.

The women wore a rainbow of sundresses, but it was pretty easy to pick out Heather, with her short red hair that the breeze picked up and tossed about her head and face. She was speaking with Monica, who pointed around the gazebo as if describing what the decorations would be. Heather was already fitting into Valentine—he wanted her to love it enough to stay.

The benches nearby were already filled with family and a few friends, including the widows. Nate talked to Father Frank, the priest from St. John's, a squat man with a receding hairline and glasses that caught the sunlight as he moved his head. Chris hung back and watched it all, like he usually did. In some ways, he'd always been an observer of life—until he'd seen Heather. Until, for the first time, he'd needed to step forward and claim something for himself.

Once everyone had arrived, Father Frank began to speak, describing the schedule for the ceremony. Everyone lined up, and as Chris already knew, he was partnered with Heather. She blushed but met his gaze. Then he stood up front with Nate and watched Heather come down the aisle, where tomorrow a long, white carpet would run between rows of chairs. The sun slanted through the trees as it neared the top of the nearest mountain, setting her hair afire, and although he should look away, appear uninterested, he couldn't.

And in his mind he was back in that hotel room, remembering how they'd sat naked in bed and talked about their lives. He already knew so much about her—the wistfulness and pride in her voice when she mentioned her brother's kids, the way she made fun of herself for being a band geek in high school and playing the trombone. And then, of course, her love affair with anything related to food. They'd ordered room service, and she'd sampled each dish, describing the specific ingredients she could taste. It was amazing what she could detect because of all her years of training.

Now she was standing with the other women in his life. She looked good there, right, and he didn't want her to leave Valentine.

As they walked back down the aisle together, he actually avoided her gaze. He was so aroused by his memories of her, that if he looked into her green eyes, everyone else would soon be able to tell just how turned on he was. He felt like a horny teenager again. He was glad when it was time to head to the Sweetheart Ranch for the rehearsal dinner. He needed a little time to compose himself before he saw her again.

Then Will offered her a ride, and without thinking, Chris almost insisted that *he* should do it, like it was his right, just because they'd slept together. He was relieved when she said she was riding with the other women, and that they all had a few things to organize before the dinner. Will gave him a strange look, as if he sensed something, but Chris only waved and started walking toward his pickup.

How was he supposed to get through the next few days, not looking at her, not touching?

Chapter Six

HEATHER LOVED HER first view of the Sweetheart Ranch, nestled in the mountain foothills just like the inn a few miles away. The two-story home itself had tall windows, and long, low additions built off both sides, all sided with dark wood. Most of the wedding party headed directly inside, chatting with excitement about the next day, but Heather found herself walking across the yard toward the huge barn with other low buildings, sheds, and trailers scattered behind it. The sun had gone behind the mountains, casting the ranch in shade, but there were still several hours before full dark. This was Chris's home, the place that had shaped him, the place he never wanted to leave.

Then she saw a lone horseman riding down the lane that separated fenced-in fields where tall grain waved in the breeze, a dog trotting smartly behind. She knew it was Chris before she even saw his face, perhaps the squareness of his shoulders, or the way he held himself so loose and at ease on the horse. He seemed at ease with everything, unlike her, who could worry with the best of them. Off behind him, several deer bounded through a distant field, but no cows grazed, which seemed strange for a ranch.

As he came closer, she saw that he wore high muddy boots over his jeans and a mud-spattered t-shirt. He tipped his hat, and she remembered that was one of the things she liked about him from the first, his gentlemanly manners.

"Hey, Heather," he said in that low, deep voice. "Long time no see."

His smile was faint, overshadowed by . . . something darker, something that called to her, a memory of curtains drawn and bodies moving together, needing only touch.

Once again she was blushing, and she glanced over her shoulder toward the house. She shouldn't linger—their connection would be too obvious to anyone watching. But she couldn't leave. It was as if someone had taken over her body to make her a woman who took risks, who lived for the danger of discovery.

Chris stood still, as if he, too, felt the dark spell she was under. Somehow she had to distract herself.

"Did you have to work between the rehearsal and the dinner?" she asked, squinting up at him against the bright blue sky.

He dismounted, keeping his hand on the horse's neck, his voice husky as he spoke. "A little. We're still irrigating our hay crop, and twice a day I have to move dams."

"Move dams?" she echoed, unable to even imagine what he meant, but glad she had something to distract herself.

He smiled. "They're made of canvas stretched across poles, so we can move them around and divert water as we need to. The hay fields need to be flooded several times before harvest. The Colorado mountains are a desert climate—if you drive around enough, you'll see some cactus. I could do the work using an ATV, but there's just something about riding a horse. Guess that's why I'm a cowboy."

The dog came closer and sat at Heather's feat, adorable with her pointy-nosed face and tongue hanging to one side. She had pointy ears, too, and a sleek, thick coat made up of browns and blacks and reds.

"Who's this?" she asked. "And does she like to be petted?"

"That's Uma, an Alaskan husky. She's a friendly girl and a hard worker."

Heather reached down and scratched the soft fur between Uma's ears, and the dog leaned into it as if with gratitude. Heather's smile faded as she looked up to find Chris watching her intently. She was caught once again in that magical connection that seemed to bond them together.

She straightened and forced herself to study the fenced-in fields. Something had already struck her as odd, but her brain was slow before it finally kicked into gear. "So where are the cows?" She felt his intense regard and wished he'd look away, but she seemed to be the only coward there.

"They spend the summer higher in the mountains, on our grazing allotment in the White River National Forest. We check up on them regularly, move them from pasture to pasture. We'll bring them down before winter."

"So right now you're growing their winter food." She glanced at him, because she couldn't resist anymore.

He nodded. "It can be dirty work, but I don't mind it. I like being alone, walking the fields, studying the water's trail and where it should go next. I find fawns bedding down by the stream, hawks and eagles rising as I ride toward hundred-year-old cottonwoods. It's beautiful countryside. And I have to enjoy it now, because when haying season starts, stress happens, with long days of hard work and fear of storms delaying the harvest, when we have to cut so much for winter."

She hadn't really thought much about what cowboys did, and frankly had assumed so much of it was mechanized in the twenty-first century. But Chris was still riding his horse, guiding cattle as had been done for hundreds of years. He was a part of ranching country, this lovely small town, and it made her ache to find her own place to fit in. Could it be Valentine Valley?

The silence became drawn out, as if neither wanted to break it. They both heard a knock on glass behind them, and turned to see Nate smiling from inside, but gesturing his impatience.

Chris deliberately turned away from the groom and stared down at her. "I don't understand what's happening to me, but I wish we could stay out here and find out."

She searched his gaze helplessly, remembering their kiss, and wanting more—even when she knew people were watching them from the house. She took a step back, and covered her mouth with her trembling hand.

He sighed. "I was going to suggest there was a hayloft I've never explored, but I guess that's out of the question now."

She gave a faint smile, glad for his attempt at humor.

"Let me unsaddle Red and I'll walk with you up to the house."

Heather found herself trailing him toward the barn, watching his stroll, unable to stop admiring the broad shoulders and narrow waist. She kept remembering him without any clothes at all, beckoning to her to join him in bed. To distract herself, she asked, "Did you like growing up on a ranch? I assume you had more chores than I did. I had to make my bed and empty the dishwasher—tough work, I know."

He laughed as he began to unbuckle the saddle. "I got to do a lot of things other kids didn't. I was guiding cattle along ridges by the time I was eight, after having saddled the horse myself. I was driving stick long before I was legally allowed to, because the cows have to get fed in winter time. I'd even delivered a calf a time or two before I was sixteen. I knew what I did was work, but it was also a matter of life or death sometimes, and everything contributed to my family's future. And kids in town never spent as much time with their dad as I did. I had fun, too, in High School Rodeo and 4-H."

He was quiet as he led his horse to feed. She remained

silent, too, distracted by the description of his childhood, of his life.

"But I love it," he said at last, as they fell in step for the walk up to the house. "Even when the sheriff calls in the middle of the night because the cows escaped and are making a run for it."

That made her laugh, and she was feeling more in control of herself as they crossed the porch and opened the front door.

Then he stopped. "My mom'll kill me if I come in like this. I'll go around back through the mud room, take a quick shower, and meet you all in a few minutes."

She watched him walk away, then with a deep breath, went inside, surprised to find the house decorated totally different than she'd imagined. There were crystals hanging in the windows to catch the last rays of the sun, tarot cards on an end table, and paintings with unicorns beside waterfalls. But the more she saw of Chris's mother, an "earth mother" if there ever was one, the more she understood.

Nate and Emily had their heads together over their glasses of wine, and both turned to look at her, as if she'd been the subject of their conversation. Heather's throat tightened with unease, and suddenly she felt like *everyone* was looking at her. Even though she knew with all logic that at most, people thought she and Chris had a flirtation going, their speculative gazes still struck too close to home.

She felt on the outside of the celebration that night, much as she tried to enjoy herself. She kept on the opposite side of the room from Chris wherever possible, yet still managed to watch him interact with his family and friends, to see how welcomed he was, how much he loved his family. It reminded her too much of the ache that never went away for her own parents who'd died so young when their tour bus crashed in England five years before.

And then Will, on seeing that Heather and Chris had been assigned seats next to each other at dinner, made a comment that she should be careful, or she'd end up the next stranger Chris tried to pick up.

Several people laughed halfheartedly even as she made a point of rolling her eyes, but Will's parents gave him a stern look. Chris actually wore a thunderous frown, a bad idea, since it caused Will to look both surprised and curious. Heather hastily took her seat, thinking all she had to get through was the wedding and reception the next day. And then . . . she could see what happened between Chris and her.

CLOSE TO MIDNIGHT, Heather stood at the sliding door to her little balcony, looking out on the rain that hid the moon and made the lights on the grounds little pinpricks in the murky darkness. She prayed the rain would be gone by morning.

She hugged herself, feeling alone and restless, her mind tirelessly going through the evening where she'd tried to enjoy the conversation, and ended up focused on *not* looking at Chris. It should have been exhausting, but she was more wired than anything else.

And then someone knocked on her door. She crossed the room with purpose, knowing who it was, knowing that the day and the evening had led to this moment.

Chris stood in the doorway, rain darkening his blond hair and soaking his buttoned-down shirt and jeans. He braced both hands on the doorway and gazed at her intently. "I know I shouldn't have come, but I've thought about no one but you for all of these months, and to know you're here, so close . . ."

His voice trailed off, and his eyes grew even more intense until they seemed to burn her.

She clasped her hands together hard to keep from touching him. "You mean people teased you about me," she breathlessly reminded him.

"It was worth it—*you* are worth it. I stood outside and tried to make myself leave you alone, and you can see where that got me. I even had to shake off my cousin, Theresa, in the lobby, and maybe you won't want to hear that. It could make her suspicious, though I think I pulled it off. If you want me to leave, just tell me."

She put her hands on his wet, whiskered face and kissed him as she'd longed to do all evening. He embraced her, lifting her off the floor, and she only vaguely heard as he kicked the door shut. Her feet didn't even brush the carpet and she barely noticed his damp clothes as they kissed with desperation, open mouths slanting together, her moans mingling with his groans.

Against her lips, he said hoarsely, "I'm getting you all wet."

"Let's get out of these clothes."

And it was like no time had passed at all since they'd last been together. They unbuttoned and unzipped and pulled apart each other's clothing, caressing and remembering. Chris bent her back over the bed, kissing his way down her breasts and stomach, and she held his head against her. And when she couldn't take it anymore, she rolled him onto his back and began her own slow exploration until he was quivering.

He groaned. "Stop, I have a condom somewhere, and I need it."

Laughing, she waited for him, then gasped when at last he crawled between her thighs and settled in, his erection cradled against the hot achy depths of her body. For just a moment, they stared into each other's eyes, humor fading.

"Heather," he whispered. "I—"

She covered his mouth. "No words, Chris. Just take me."

He entered her so slowly, his expression intent, as if he meant to experience every delicious second of pleasure. She moved beneath him restlessly, wanting to pull him in all the way, yet enjoying the desperation, too, as well as her rising need. When at last he surged deep inside her, she was overwhelmed by an orgasm that left her shuddering.

"Damn, I'm good," he said hoarsely.

Her laugh was also a moan of satisfaction. He began to move inside her, and before she knew it, she was keeping pace with his arousal, straining to merge with him, to be one with him, to experience the pleasure again, but this time together.

Afterward, as their breathing began to calm, he rolled to his side and she did the same, so that he could spoon behind her.

His kissed her shoulder and murmured, "I could stay here forever."

"And how would that look?" she answered slowly, sleepily.

He hesitated. "I know you care—I care, too, I promise. I tried not to come here, tried to spare you the worry of discovery. I think I made a good enough excuse to my cousin about why I was here, but . . ."

She sighed and held his hand against her breast. "You must think I'm being ridiculous in this day and age."

He hugged her tightly for a moment. "I would never think that. I know just how it feels to receive curious looks."

"Because of me."

"I don't remember you dragging me kicking and screaming. We were both in that hotel room together."

She squirmed until she was on her back looking up at him, then brushed a lock of hair from his eyes. "It's just that . . . Emily means so much to me—to us both. She's been my closest friend, and I miss her a lot. Part of me knows she'd be understanding. I—I kind of told her about the fling. Not the airport or anything," she hastened to add, and was relieved when he laughed. "She didn't judge me, of course, but now . . . you're her brother, and this is her wedding weekend, and she's already so stressed. She's doing her best not to show it, but come on, brides want everything to be perfect. I just don't want all this"—she waved an arm around—"to come out right now, bringing up past gossip."

"I get that," he said gently.

"This is a small town, and I know small towns. One of the things I love is how close people are, how much they care and help each other. But close people sometimes feel like that entitles them to any sort of gossip."

"So you're going to leave and make me chase you across the country," he teased.

She smiled. "I didn't say that. I . . ." How could she tell him that she'd agreed to allow Emily to show her around town in the morning, that Emily had contacted a real estate office about buildings for sale? It would give him hope, and she wasn't sure that was fair. "I just need a little time."

"I understand." He kissed her forehead. "And though I'm going to regret it the rest of the night, I have to go. I'll take the back way to avoid Theresa." He slid to a sitting position on the edge of the bed to pull on his jeans. Once he was dressed, he braced himself on one arm and leaned down for a final kiss. "I thought I'd never be with you again," he whispered. "This has been better than all my fantasies of a reunion."

She smiled softly. "For me, too."

When he left, she lay still a long time, looking at the door, her smile fading. She'd just made it even harder to pretend a casual acquaintanceship with him at the wedding tomorrow. But she didn't regret it.

Chapter Seven

HEATHER ENJOYED HER early morning time with Emily, who drove up and down every street in Valentine Valley, pointing out eclectic stores and restaurants, doing her best to entice Heather to stay.

Howie Deering Jr., the real estate agent, met them at a building on Grace Street, literally on the other side of Emily's block. An alley ran between the row of storefronts where Sugar and Spice and Monica's Flowers and Gifts sat by side, and the old-fashioned houses facing the other way. The available old Victorian was on the corner of Grace and Second, behind Wine Country—which Emily insisted would come in handy in their small, nosy town.

Heather smiled weakly, and if Emily noticed, she didn't say anything.

When they were done walking through the house that had most recently been a shoe repair shop before the owner expanded, they retreated to Sugar and Spice, so Heather could ooh and aah over the kitchen.

When they came out into the front room, the freckle-faced teenage girl manning the counter gaped at them.

"Emily, it's your wedding day!" she practically shrieked.

Several customers, who were browsing the display cases full of pastries, turned to gape.

Emily raised both hands. "It's okay, Karista, I'm just here for a quick hot chocolate. I have plenty of time."

Karista put a hand to her chest and breathed heavily. "OMG, I thought you were calling it off. And that Nate is so hot!"

Heather covered her mouth to hide a smile at the girl's theatrics. Karista normally worked for Monica's Flowers and Gifts, but she'd agreed to help Emily during the wedding weekend.

"I think he's hot, too," Emily said patiently. "When you get a chance, could you bring me a hot chocolate and Heather a coffee?"

Heather grimaced as they sat down at the little two-person table. "Hot chocolate in the summer?"

"You drink coffee in the summer, don't you?"

Heather couldn't argue with that. She gazed around at the bakery, full of summer flowers and tiny little wedding bells at each table.

Emily saw where she was looking and winced. "The widows' idea. They work here. They thought every customer should know I was getting married. If it was up to them, I'd have been wearing a veil on my head this entire week."

Heather smiled. "Did you bake your own wedding cake?"

"I get asked that a lot, and yeah, I did, although it isn't an elaborately decorated creation. There are several cakes for several different tastes."

"Yum, can I have some of each?"

"I hope you're the only one with that sentiment, or there won't be enough for everyone."

"All right, all right, I'll restrain myself," she said, smiling up at Karista who placed her coffee on the table. Heather added cream and sugar and took a welcome sip. "Delicious."

"Thanks. I learned the best brands from you." Emily stirred her hot chocolate idly as she eyed Heather. "Tell me you'll consider buying that house and that you'll move to Valentine Valley. Surely you've fallen in love with it."

"I—"

"Think of everything you could do for the lovers who descend on our town all year. You could give classes on making romantic meals, or offer gourmet dinners just for two, set up right in the customer's home or hotel room. You could—"

"Wait!" Heather held up a hand, laughing. "You're getting ahead of yourself."

"You're right, I am. So tell me why you're letting your last boyfriend chase you out of San Francisco."

Heather sighed. "I'm not, really I'm not. You know the city makes me crazy. I feel . . . anonymous, and also overwhelmed with the stress of trying to find customers when there are so many chefs who do what I do, and maybe do it better."

Emily waved a hand. "That's ridiculous. Your food is exquisite."

Heather hesitated, then spoke in a quiet voice. "At first I did worry that Andrew was ruining the city for me. I was letting him and my surprise at the shallowness of our relationship affect everything I did. But I'm over that, I swear. And one thing I've learned—I will never again let a man influence my opinion. I make my own decisions now."

"Well, I'm glad to hear that. But I've still been worried about you ever since you arrived."

Heather felt a ripple of unease that she worked to suppress. "Worried? What have I done to make you feel that way? I'm having a wonderful time in Valentine."

"You're trying hard, I know. But something's going on, and it's not Andrew."

Heather said nothing. She was worried if she started speaking, words would tumble out uncontrollably. She refused to burden Emily on her wedding day.

"Oh come on, Heather! I think a symptom of your problem is that you and my brother are doing a little flirting."

Heather studied her friend carefully, but it seemed an innocent statement. "Flirting?"

"Even Nate has noticed, and trust me, he's usually oblivious to that sort of thing. Flirting doesn't hurt anyone, but if something's going on with you, maybe it's a sign of something deeper."

A sign of something deeper? Heather almost laughed. "Emily, I would never want to distract you from having the best wedding weekend. This is nothing, honestly. I just don't know anyone but you, and Chris has been nice."

Emily crossed her arms over her chest and gave her a mock frown. "You're not going to say anything more? I like details, you know."

"There's nothing to say, honestly. Now don't we have a wedding to prepare for? Decorations to set up at the inn?"

Emily eyed her a moment longer, then shook her head, her expression a little disappointed. "You're a tough nut to crack lately, Heather Armstrong. But I'm not finished trying."

DRESSED IN A summer-blue cocktail dress, Heather felt all eyes on her as she walked down the carpeted aisle in the mid-afternoon sunlight. Behind her, the other bridesmaids wore the same color, but in a style of dress that suited each of them best. A string quartet played inside the gazebo, where white bunting had been strung along the railings. Flowers festooned the gazebo, and were also attached to each white folding chair that lined the white-carpet aisle.

And standing beside the gazebo stairs, the groom looked handsome in his suit, along with each of his ushers. Nate Thalberg gave the appearance of a man who was about to have everything he wanted in life: a lover, a partner, a wife. He smiled at Heather, and she smiled back, lips trembling. Next she glanced at Chris, and his blue eyes looked at her so warmly that she knew she was reddening as she lowered her gaze back to the carpet. She could almost feel him kissing her, touching her, but banished the memories so she wouldn't trip on her way up the aisle.

As she took her place opposite the ushers, she turned to watch each of the bridesmaids make their own way toward her, carrying casual bouquets of daisies: Brooke Thalberg, sister of the groom, and Monica Shaw, good friend of the bride. Heck, Brooke was the bride's friend, too. Heather knew that both women had welcomed Emily to Valentine, befriended her, helped her in her quest to find her lost family and a home. Emily's teenage sister Steph came last, and the girl's eyes glistened with tears even as she smiled proudly to everyone she knew. A ripple of chuckles moved through the crowd as one by one, people saw the cowboy boots Steph sported proudly.

Heather imagined Emily, hidden within a white tent, was having a hard time holding back her own tears, since she'd discovered her true family only a year ago, and now they were all in her wedding. It was what Emily had wanted, a real family.

When she emerged from the tent on the arm of her dad, Joe Sweet, he beamed down at her with all the love a father could bestow. Nate straightened his shoulders resolutely, wearing a look of pride and love. The crowd gasped at the sight of the bride and rose as one, as the string quartet broke into a very interesting but recognizable version of "At Last."

Heather exchanged teary smiles with the other three

bridesmaids. In her mind, she sang the next line of the lyric, *My love has come along . . .* and it took everything in her not to glance at Chris. *Could he be her love?* Did it happen that fast, with just one look at each other? How was she supposed to know—to trust in happily-ever-afters? She'd been so certain she'd had that once before. *But Chris wasn't Andrew,* she thought resolutely. And after last night, and the helpless way she fell into Chris's arms, how could she continue kidding herself?

Emily continued her slow walk down the aisle, the train of her gown trailing behind, smiling at all her guests, no tears in her eyes, only an expression of joy and happiness. She hugged her father's arm tight and grinned up at him.

Joe Sweet was Chris's father, too, his longish hair blonde streaked with white, yet as tall and strapping a cowboy as his sons. He'd spent his life on the land, and made such a powerful impression on his sons that Chris wanted the same thing for himself. And Heather had to admit she liked a man who knew what he wanted.

And Chris seemed to want her.

When Emily and Nate faced each other, the priest behind and above them on the stairs of the gazebo, they pledged their vows with confidence and tenderness. Heather had to breathe deeply to stop her tears from falling. She well remembered how unhappy Emily had been in her old life, in her old marriage, but that had never stopped her from supporting Heather with understanding and cheerfulness. To see her have the happiness she so deserved was something Heather had prayed for.

When the priest pronounced them husband and wife, he didn't even get out the words "You may kiss the bride," before Nate and Emily stepped into each other's arms and shared a passionate yet tender kiss. The guests burst into wild applause, which continued when the happy couple grinned at everyone, then looked into each other's eyes as if they could see the wonderful future already stretching before them. Holding hands, they practically ran down the aisle while friends and family threw birdseed.

And then it was time to meet up with Chris for her own walk down the aisle, the last two in the wedding party. He held out his elbow and she slid her hand into his warmth, then smiled at the guests instead of meeting those intense blue eyes. But his arm felt so good in hers, and suddenly she wished he was holding her.

One more day, she told herself. *I just have to get through this one day. And then I'll figure everything out—or start to, anyway.*

They spent time posing for pictures in the park and on the banks of Silver Creek. The family had even brought along Nate's horse, Apollo, so Nate could sweep Emily off her feet the old-fashioned way. Heather's favorite photo was captured just as the setting sun was slanting through the gazebo. Emily stood against Nate, her bouquet dangling from her hand, her eyes closed in happy contentment, while he kissed her forehead.

When the wedding party reached the Sweetheart Inn, the other wedding guests were already sampling appetizers and cocktails on the terrace, while the sun set behind the mountains. Gradually, everyone moved inside to the banquet room where two walls of windows framed the beautiful view. Heather had helped the rest of the bridesmaids set up for the wedding reception that morning with Emily—the floating candles, the pictures of Nate and Emily strung on a clothesline behind the wedding cakes which were perched atop tiny, cut sections of tree trunks. Each guest received a mason jar with the dry ingredients of Emily's famous chocolate chip cookies, a well-guarded secret recipe. Candles and flowers decorated the room, with extra flowers heaped before Nate and Emily's private table.

When the bride and groom were introduced, they whirled into their own dance to Bryan Adams's "Everything I Do, I Do It For You." The wedding party was supposed to join in, and Heather found herself walking toward Chris. She slid into his arms with a feeling of rightness. Though some of the others might be talking and laughing, even clowning for the crowd, she couldn't. Being held in Chris's embrace seemed too important for words as they stared at each other. Then he smiled, and so did she, and they spun across the floor.

Chris gazed down into Heather's green eyes and almost forgot that his sister had just gotten married. Oh, he'd enjoyed the ceremony at the gazebo, and knew his sister would be happy with Nate, a man he'd admired his entire life. He was a few years younger than Nate, and there'd been a time when he thought the other man a little too perfect, but now "perfect" was just right for Emily.

Emily was the reason he could at last hold Heather in

his arms again. His sister had brought Heather to Valentine, when Chris had never thought to see her again. He wasn't going to let her go, not after the evening they'd shared last night. Somehow he had to find a way to convince her that she could make a life here—with him. And if that was too fast for her, he had no problem doing an old-fashioned courtship until she really understood that she was no temporary fling.

After dinner, he enjoyed watching Heather with the other bridesmaids as they all followed Steph's lead and switched into cowboy boots for the dancing. They had a bluegrass band that covered everything from Pink Floyd to Johnny Cash, and the women kicked up their heels, while the photographer and the guests snapped lots of photos. Heather didn't dance with him again, and he understood. She wanted this day to be for Emily, and he did, too. Tomorrow he'd talk to her about their future. Or maybe later tonight.

He saw the photographer pin a microphone to Emily's dress, but when he didn't hear her voice over the band, he assumed it was to be used a little later. He was sipping a beer on the outskirts of the dance floor when his older brother approached.

"You're not dancing much," Will said after swigging his own beer. "But then you usually don't." He grinned.

Chris smiled back and continued to watch the dance floor.

"What do you think about Em's friend, Heather?"

Wary, Chris kept his expression neutral. "I like her. She's nice."

"I like her, too. In fact, I think I might do something about it."

Chris glanced at Will, but spoke mildly to hide his irritation. "You mean ask her to dance?"

"Naw, maybe to go out tonight after the reception."

"That's probably not a good idea."

And that was the wrong thing to say. Will focused an interested gaze on him, as if he'd hoped for such a reaction.

"And why not? She's unattached, according to Em."

Chris said nothing—and even found himself grinding his teeth. He knew his behavior was suspicious, but he just couldn't stop himself. Now that he'd found Heather, he'd be damned if he'd watch his own brother hit on her.

"Or is there something about Heather you're not telling me?" Will continued, elbowing him. "Come on, I'm your big brother—who else can you tell your secrets to? You're hot for her, aren't you?"

"Look, it's none of your business, Will. Let it go."

"Okay, then I'll just go over and make her happy."

Chris caught his arm. "Don't."

"Don't?" Will echoed. "You act as if you have some proprietary right over her."

"That's not true."

"Oh yes, it is. It's as if you've met her before or . . ." Will's eyes widened. "You *have* met her before, haven't you?"

Chris wished he had Will's easy way with a lie, but he didn't, so all he could do was say nothing.

Will suddenly gaped at Heather, now part of a conga

line with the bridesmaids and other guests. "She's your redheaded airport lover, isn't she?"

"Shut up," Chris said between clenched teeth.

And then to make it worse, he heard a gasp, and turned around to find Emily just behind them, her expression one of surprise and . . . something else.

"Don't say anything more!" she said urgently.

"Em—" he began, but she put up a hand.

"I'll talk to you later," she promised.

She marched between them, almost elbowing them aside as she made a bee-line directly for Heather.

Chris groaned and briefly closed his eyes. "Now look what you've done," he muttered to Will.

"Me?" Will said, spreading his arms wide.

Chris ignored his brother, trying to decide if he should interfere. Emily and Heather were friends, and Emily didn't look angry, only sort of . . . intent. People were applauding as the music faded away, but it all seemed distant to him as Emily took both of Heather's upper arms in her hands and spoke quietly. He winced as Heather's expression wrinkled in shock and dismay.

There was a crackle of the sound system, and then suddenly the microphone on Emily's neckline clearly picked up Heather's words and transmitted them through the whole reception.

"But we were snowed in at the airport, and it just happened!"

Chapter Eight

HEATHER HEARD HER own words ringing loudly through the entire banquet room. And then there was nothing but dead silence.

Emily's face was pale, her expression full of remorse as she yanked off the microphone and glared at it as if it were a snake.

Heather was afraid to move, afraid to gaze anywhere but at Emily. She'd wanted more than anything for her best friend to have the wedding of her dreams. And instead Emily was finding out that Heather had already "met" her brother. She'd been worried the secret would come out, and she'd done it all to herself. And now everybody knew, including the groom's parents and grandparents and—

She squeezed her eyes shut. "Oh, God," she whispered.

"Don't look like that!" Emily whispered excitedly. "You have no idea how happy this makes me—I literally schemed to keep the two of you together this weekend because I thought you were perfect for each other!"

They gaped at each other, and Heather felt a bubble of hysterical laughter rise in her throat.

"Heather!" Chris's voice boomed across the dance floor.

She choked off her laughter and felt herself pale. Emily squeezed her hand.

"You could at least tell her the whole story. I begged you to meet me in Denver, regardless of how bad the weather was."

She slowly raised her gaze to him, and his handsome, concerned face was like a lifeline tossed to her as she sank amid her own mistakes.

"I know I told you I didn't want anyone to know about us until I knew what you wanted of me," he said, walking slowly toward her. "And it was the hardest thing I've ever done, letting people think that I'd picked you up as if you were only a stranger, when I'd already known for months that you were the only woman for me."

"Why did you let them think that?" she said weakly, then cleared her throat. "I wouldn't have asked it of you."

He took both her hands in his and bent to kiss the back of each one. "What we have together is more important to me than what people think, so I let it go. I was ready to wait until you made a decision about me, but I wasn't going to give you *that* much time. You're too special to me. I love you, Heather."

He sounded clear and so impassioned that she almost believed him.

Oh God, she *wanted* to believe him. How was that possible?

"I was going to tell you that in the airport when I came to pick you up, but then Emily arrived." He gave his sister an apologetic smile. "I couldn't tell *you*, Em, not until I'd talked to Heather."

"As if I'd mind," Emily scoffed.

She wore a broad and satisfied smile as if she'd had a hand in it all. To think she'd thought she was matchmaking for two strangers!

She positively beamed at Heather. "I think your relationship is absolutely wonderful. My brother and one of my best friends. Could my wedding be any more complete?"

Heather felt a lump in her throat the size of Colorado, and she gazed at Emily with love and gratitude.

Then Emily looked around. "Where's the music? It's time to dance and celebrate! Nate, put that beer down. We're not at Tony's Tavern watching a game of pool. Get on over here!"

"If we were at Tony's," Nate drawled as he ambled over, "I'd already be gettin' a kiss from you right now. That place just does something to you."

Emily giggled and let Nate drag her back out on the dance floor.

Heather continued to hold Chris's hands and stare up at him in disbelief. All around them, voices rose in a buzz, and one or two couples made their way to the dance floor as the first bars of Journey's "Faithfully" began. She knew the two of them were still the main object of curiosity, but Chris had sweetly made everyone think they didn't know the whole story.

"Let's get out of here," he said, pulling on her hands.

Looking only at him, she allowed him to lead her out the French doors onto the terrace. Though the sun had long since set, there were lampposts scattered along the stone balustrade, so she could see the tenderness in his expression.

"Oh, Chris, I'm so sorry. I've caused you nothing but trouble ever since we met." She gestured toward the banquet room. "In there, you were . . . you were magnificent. But you didn't have to do that, to lie to your family and friends."

He slid his arms around her waist and linked them at her back. "I don't care what they think, darlin'. I'd do anything for you. That snowstorm was the best thing that ever happened to me, and I wouldn't change a thing."

"But . . . you said you loved me. You shouldn't have. They'll think—"

"They're not important—you are. And I wasn't lying, not one bit." His voice dropped into huskiness. "I *do* love you, Heather. After we went our separate ways, I couldn't think of anything else—didn't *want* anyone else. To find you again has been like a dream for me. Say you'll move here. Say you'll be with me."

"Should I say I love you first?" she whispered.

He hesitated, and for the first time looked uncertain. "Only if you want to."

She cupped his face in her hands. "I love you, Chris. I

can't believe I'm saying it so fast, but I believe it with my whole heart. And everything's fast with us."

He grinned and kissed the tip of her nose.

"The moment I met you," she continued, "I was drawn to you in a way I'd never thought possible. You brought out someone brave in me, made me step beyond the careful, cheerless world I'd made for myself in San Francisco. And I love it here in Valentine almost as much as I love you."

He hugged her then, whirling her around. Then somehow voices lifted in song wafting from the banquet room penetrated their happiness.

He set her down and kissed her again, then glanced at the partially open doors. "Did you hear that? It doesn't sound like the band."

"Much as I'd love to stay out here forever, we *are* part of the bridal party."

Arm in arm, they went to the doorway and paused with wonder. The three widows of the Widows' Boardinghouse were standing at a microphone, singing an old-fashioned song in three-part harmony—and changing the words to represent Nate and Emily. The guests were enthralled, women—and men—openly wiping away tears.

"They sing beautifully," Heather whispered.

Emily kept her arm around Nate, tears making glistening streaks down her face. Heather knew how much Emily had appreciated the widows treating her like their own granddaughter.

"This must be their special surprise for the wedding," Heather said.

Chris moved behind her and linked his arms around her waist, swaying to the music. She leaned back against him, feeling at peace, perhaps for the first time in her life. She had a future to look forward to—and a wonderful man to love.

Epilogue

THE BEAUTIFUL SONG wasn't the only surprise from the widows. At the end of the reception, the toot of an old-fashioned car horn called everyone out to the terrace, where a 1920s roadster with the top down sat rumbling in the drive.

"It's the perfect way to leave your reception!" Mrs. Thalberg called to her grandson and his new wife.

"We bought it to drive in parades," Mrs. Palmer drawled, a tiara perched on her big blond wig. "I'll look real cute in costume drivin' it along—but I'm glad you two get to use it first!"

Wedding guests gathered to watch Nate and Emily leave, but the newly married couple stopped in front of Heather and Chris first.

"Is everything okay?" Emily asked with hope in her voice.

"Now don't pressure them," Nate said.

"That's okay." Heather grinned. "Everything is wonderful—better than I ever imagined. Em, you don't mind me stealing your brother, do you?"

Emily laughed. "I think it's just perfect!"

Nate clasped Chris's hand, shaking his head briefly as if in amusement, before lifting his wife clear off the ground to carry her toward the waiting car.

There were shouts and cheers, and when Chris's father was done waving good-bye, he turned and looked right at them.

Heather stiffened. "Do you think—"

But Joe Sweet only grinned and nudged his wife.

Faith simply laughed and laughed, before getting her breath back enough to call, "Never a dull moment in Valentine Valley, Heather—I'll just warn you now!"

Heather clung to Chris's hand and smiled up at him with tenderness. "I wouldn't have it any other way!"

Can't get enough of Valentine Valley?
Good news, there is so much more to come!
Hollywood's former bad girl has arrived in
Valentine Valley—
can the resident cowboy tame her heart?
Keep reading for a sneak peek of

THE COWBOY OF VALENTINE VALLEY

coming in February 2014 . . .

An Excerpt from

THE COWBOY OF VALENTINE VALLEY

WHITNEY WINSLOW SAT on the patio of The Adelaide Bed and Breakfast, trying to get her thoughts in order— trying to avoid the thrill of excitement deep in the pit of her stomach as she awaited the arrival of Josh Thalberg, Colorado cowboy and designer of some of the most exquisite leatherwork she'd ever seen. The August air was scented with Columbines, warm without being too hot, as it often was in the mountains surrounding Valentine Valley. The fountain gurgled nearby, a fish jumped in the pond, but none of it relaxed Whitney as she nervously touched her hair and tugged on her pencil skirt. She'd dressed for a business meeting so Josh would understand their professional relationship, though she'd been the one to make it all personal eight months ago, right in this very B&B.

Then it was too late for regrets. Josh emerged from the garden path, tall and lanky, and she couldn't stop herself from drinking everything in, from his cowboy boots, up his faded jeans, to the western plaid shirt that covered broad shoulders. He had a worn backpack hanging from one shoulder and held his Stetson against his thigh, leaving his dark brown hair tousled appealingly. The faint shadow of a couple days' growth of beard didn't hide the curved scar on his chin, evidence of the sometimes dangerous work he did on the Silver Creek Ranch. He had a straight, perfect nose, and the cheekbones any male model would envy. But his eyes captured her the most, hazel and changeable as swirling mist, but full of warmth and amusement—and, surprisingly, interest, as they swept over her body in return.

A thrill of heat followed wherever his gaze touched. Who'd known she would feel like this? She'd always thought a man was sexiest in an expensive tailored suit, but ever since she'd first arrived in Valentine Valley, worn jeans and broken-in cowboy boots were doing it for her.

Josh arched a dark brow, a hint of the devil in his smile. "Nice to see you again, Whitney."

His deep drawl still gave her the shivers.

She stood up. "You, too, Josh," she said, proud that her voice didn't betray her nerves.

She was never nervous! Why did he make her feel this way?

His eyes grew almost smoky as he studied her. Tension shimmered between them, promising possibilities that she didn't want to face. It had been a long time since her own behavior had embarrassed her, but now it was hard to forget what a fool she'd made of herself.

His expression full of interest and speculation, he said, "You've been gone a long time."

She shrugged. "Business and family. You know how it is."

Well, the family part wasn't really true. Her parents had wanted to spend Christmas in Rio, so Whitney, her brother Chasz, and his wife, Camilla, had joined them, but only for a week. Then Whitney had gone back to work. She loved her growing stores, her line of lingerie known just by her first name. She was usually so focused on making herself a success—but to her dismay, Josh hadn't been far from her thoughts.

"So I wasn't the one who drove you away?" he asked.

She quickly shook her head. "I wanted to give Valentine Valley time to get used to the idea of my store." She'd been letting things die down after the protests that had split the little mountain town over whether Leather and Lace, her upscale lingerie store, could be classified as pornography and banned from opening. She'd persuaded the town council to her side, but she hadn't done it alone.

The Thalbergs and their friends had rallied around her. Josh, beloved local son, had agreed to do some leather tooling for her, which had probably gotten her even more sympathy and maybe carried the day. And she'd almost ruined their business relationship before it began. "And as for you driving me away? My own behavior was at fault, not you. I got a little drunk and pushy—"

"You weren't pushy," he interrupted, wearing that easy grin that did things to her insides. "You were sexy as all hell."

"But I was drunk, and you were gracious when you turned me down." The first man to ever refuse her offer of intimacy. "I appreciate it."

"It took all of my restraint," he said in a low voice.

She gave a heavy swallow, followed by a false smile. "Now you're just teasing me. Let's forget about it, okay?"

"Forget? No. Ignore? Okay. For a while, maybe."

"No maybes. Let's concentrate on work."

Work, the story of her life. She thought about the men she'd dated, who, just like her, were interested in nothing but an occasional dinner together, followed by a private evening of fun. No expectations, no commitments. It suited everyone involved.

But there was something about Josh and this small town that made her think that kind of anonymous pleasure wasn't possible. Another reason not to like Valentine Valley.

"Have a seat." She sat down, gesturing to the wrought-iron chair across the little table from her. "You said you'd have some sketches of the leather collar necklaces for me when I returned?"

He frowned at her as he sank into the chair. "I thought we were going to discuss what you had in mind for the designs, and then I'd draw some up. Did I get that wrong?"

"It doesn't matter now," she said, regretting the miscommunication. "We'll just move forward."

"I did bring some leather samples." He pulled the backpack off his shoulder and unzipped it. He brought out several strips of leather, different thicknesses, colors, textures, then laid them across the table so she could see them better, all the while talking about vegetable tanning to get the right tooling leather. His explanations were hard to follow when all she could think about was that this leather would be used alongside her lingerie. It was erotic and stimulating, and she began to perspire. He asked something, and she almost jumped.

"Pardon me?"

His smile was far too knowing. "I asked if these samples would be okay."

"Yes, of course. Whatever you think would work best."

"Well, you know your clients and their tastes."

She swallowed heavily. "I do."

"When do you plan to open the store?"

"I'll be consulting with the architects who put in renovation bids in the next week or two before negotiating the contract for the building." As an aside, she added, "You do know the space used to belong to a funeral home? I think I need to make it drastically different, so people forget."

He nodded, one side of his mouth still curled with amusement—at what she was saying? Or how she was behaving? She didn't know.

With mock seriousness, he said, "You know we country folk don't all believe in ghosts."

"Your grandmother's friend, Mrs. Palmer, reads tarot cards," Whitney pointed out. "Surely *she* does."

"I never asked her."

She must be stoking his amusement, so she cleared her throat and made an effort to slow down her speech. "I don't have a date in mind yet, but a grand opening just before the holidays would be ideal. If I approve the designs, can you have stock for me by then?"

"I'm not worried about you approving the designs."

"Confident, aren't you?"

He grinned. "I am. You chose me for a reason."

Now *that* could be taken several ways.

"But as for the amount of goods I can provide, I'll do what I can." For the first time, his expression turned serious. "This isn't my major business, and I never meant it to be. I hope you can be patient while I figure out how to work everything in, decide what my focus should be."

"Surely your family can help you out on the ranch."

He crossed his arms over his chest and cocked his head. "It's not as if they're sitting around watching me work."

"I remember you telling me you hired Adam Desantis, your sister's boyfriend, to help prepare leather. Is that going well?"

"He learns fast. And yes, he's been a great asset. But the tooling itself takes up the most of my time. Don't worry; I've agreed to do work for you, and I'll make it happen."

Josh had thought things would be awkward between them, and he'd been proven right. She looked ready to bolt, hands on the dainty table to push herself to her feet. She seemed to regret that her advances had altered things between them, as if she thought he didn't want her. Nothing could be further from the truth. He hadn't been able to forget about her as the months had dragged by, dwelling on the confident sexiness of her kiss, the press of her body against his, the way she excited him as no other woman ever had. It was like he'd come alive to the unimagined possibilities of sensuality. She was all understated sophistication, and moved with an easy elegance that seemed feminine and bold at the same time, if such a thing were possible.

As for turning her down? It had been the right thing to do. He was determined to have her without alcohol clouding their relationship.

But being back at the same B&B where they'd kissed? It both aroused and frustrated him, because it was obvious she was no longer in a romantic mood.

"So did you go home these last few months?" he asked. "And where is home?"

He watched her try to decide how to answer him about her private life, what he deserved to know, and knew he was intruding, but he'd never felt so curious before.

"I spent some of my childhood in San Francisco, some in Manhattan, the main headquarters of my father's company, Winslow Enterprises," she said slowly, as if reluctant. "My parents liked to travel, so we were never in one place for long."

He was surprised how fascinated he was by her background, when her looks were enough to make him tongue-tied. She was on the tall side, with a model's slimness, but with the important curves she'd pressed against his body. He tried to shake off the memory. "That must have been difficult, new schools and all."

"I went to boarding school, so that never changed."

He frowned. "You lived away from your family?"

"Just like Harry Potter but without the magic," she said with a touch of mild sarcasm.

"So your family is wealthy."

She nodded without elaborating. That explained why she chose such classy clothes, which looked like they'd been made just for her, all expensive fabrics and subtle sophistication. He liked her hair, too, shiny black, but cut in layers about her face and to her shoulders. Every time she moved, it swung and flowed with her, settling back into place to perfectly frame her delicate features and wide gray eyes. Her mouth spoiled the spare lines of her bone structure with a ripe fullness he'd tasted and hadn't been able to forget.

"So with all that traveling, your parents didn't sell your house," he said, wanting to listen to her talk.

She shook her head. "My parents have several homes."

"Around the world, I take it. Valentine must seem pretty small to you."

"I've been in many small towns, and they always have their own charm."

"Tactful response. So you set your first store in San Francisco because you knew it well." He leaned forward and rested his elbows on his knees. "But why lingerie?"

"Why not?"

She smiled again, and he knew that wasn't the whole story, and she wasn't about to enlighten him.

"I thought maybe you stayed away from Valentine because of your other stores."

"Only partly. I have good managers and a great personal assistant. In fact, I plan to have things so well run someday, I can oversee everything from Europe, where I'd like to work on establishing new stores."

He appreciated her ambition, even though a small part of him was . . . disappointed in her traveling plans. "I've never been to Europe, but I hear the snowboarding is incredible. I've explored a lot of famous western resorts out here. My friends and I take a ski vacation every year. Next February, we might try Tahoe. Sounds like your kind of place. Will I see you there?"

She chuckled. "Now you've warned me off. You don't like to travel besides the snowboarding trips?"

"I'm too busy and I have everything I need right here." She was relaxing with him, and that was better than the charged awkwardness when he'd first arrived. "So I hear I'll see you tomorrow night at the Widows' Boardinghouse. Grandma says she invited you. You'll come?"

She nodded.

"Then it's a date." He slapped his hands on his knees as he rose to his feet.

"It's not a date," she answered dryly. "But before you go, let's finalize the design ideas for your sketches."

She looked at him with that direct, confident gaze of hers. She thought she had everything under control, but he didn't see it that way. He hadn't been able to forget her these last few months, and by her very resistance, he suspected she felt the same. He could be patient. He sat back down.

After all, if he could be patient after their first kiss, when he'd been so turned on he could think of nothing but her body beneath him, then he could do anything.

They spent another half hour discussing floral designs versus geometric, subtle versus bold, and even whether a hint of animals was suggestive of sexy wildness or simply farm life. She was easy to talk to and definitely had her vision of Leather and Lace well established. He'd sketch her samples of everything they'd discussed, and go from there.

"Thanks for the explanations, Josh." She rose to her feet and looked at him expectantly, crossing her arms beneath her breasts, so that the expensive silk clearly outlined the straps of her bra.

After standing up, he smiled at her over his shoulder as he headed for the slate path through the garden. "Do you need a ride tomorrow night?"

"No, thanks, I have a rental car."

"Then I'll see you at the boardinghouse."

Her cell phone rang, and she glanced down at the table, already distancing herself. He inhaled with regret, gave her a nod, and walked away, just like he had last December.

Things were going to be different this time.

*Keep reading for a look at where it all began
in*

A TOWN CALLED VALENTINE

and

TRUE LOVE AT SILVER CREEK RANCH

Available Now!

An Excerpt from

A TOWN CALLED VALENTINE

THE CAR GAVE one last shudder as Emily Murphy came to a stop in a parking space just beneath the blinking sign of Tony's Tavern. She turned off the ignition and leaned back against the headrest as the rain drummed on the roof, and the evening's darkness settled around her. The car will be all right, she told herself firmly. Taking a deep breath, she willed her shoulders to relax after a long, stressful day driving up into the Colorado Rockies. Though the trip had been full of stunning mountain vistas still topped by snow in May, she had never let her focus waver from her mission.

She glanced up at the flashing neon sign, and her stomach growled. The tavern was near the highway and wasn't the most welcoming place. There were only two pickups and a motorcycle beside her car on this wet night.

Her stomach gurgled again, and with a sigh, she tugged up the hood of her raincoat, grabbed her purse, and stepped out into the rain. Gingerly jumping over puddles, she made it beneath the overhang above the door and went inside. A blast of heat and the smell of beer hit her face. The tavern was sparsely furnished, with a half dozen tables and a long bar on the right side of the room. Between neon signs advertising beer, mounted animal heads peered down at the half dozen customers. A man and a woman sat at one table, watching a baseball game on the flat screen TV—at least there was one other woman in the place. Another couple of men hunched at the bar, glancing from beneath their cowboy hats at her before turning away. No surprise there.

When she hesitated, the bartender, a man in his thirties, with shaggy dark hair and pleasant features, gave her a nod. "Sit anywhere you'd like."

Smiling gratefully, she slipped off her raincoat, hung it on one of the many hooks near the door, and sat down. She discovered her table was opposite the only man at a table by himself. He was directly in her line of vision, making it hard to notice anything else. He was tall, by the length of his denim-clad legs. Beneath the shadowing brim of his cowboy hat, she could see an angular face and the faint lines at the corner of his eyes of a man who spent much of his day squinting in the sun. She thought he might be older than her thirty years but not by much.

When he tipped his hat back and met her eyes, Emily gave a start, realizing she'd been caught staring. It had been so long since she'd looked at any man but her ex-husband. Her face got hot, and she quickly pulled the slightly sticky menu out from its place between a napkin dispenser and a condiment basket.

A shadow loomed over her, and for a moment, she thought she'd given the cowboy some kind of signal. Maybe her presence alone in a bar late at night was enough.

But it was only the bartender, who gave her a tired smile. "Can I get you something to drink?"

She almost said a Diet Coke, but the weariness of the day overtook her, and she found herself ordering a beer. She studied the menu while he was gone, remembered her lack of funds, and asked for a burger when he returned. Some protein, some carbs, and with lettuce and tomato, it made a pretty well-rounded meal. She had to laugh at herself.

"I didn't know the menu was that funny," said a deep voice.

Not the bartender. Emily glanced up and met the solitary cowboy's gaze. Even from one table over, she could see the gleam of his green eyes. His big hand lifted a can of beer to his lips, yet he never stopped watching her.

Was a cowboy trying to pick her up in a mountain bar? She blinked at him and tried to contain her smile. "No, I was smiling at something else," she said, trying to sound polite but cool.

To her surprise, the cowboy simply nodded, took another swig of his beer, and glanced back at the TV. She did the same, drinking absentmindedly and trying to pretend she liked baseball. Her ex-husband had been a fan of the San Francisco Giants, so she'd gone to an occasional game when one of the partners couldn't attend.

By the time her hamburger arrived, she'd finished her beer. The cowboy was watching her again, and she recklessly ordered another. Why not? Though she hadn't eaten much today, the burger would certainly offset the alcohol. Hungrily, she dug in. The two men at the bar started to play darts, and she watched them for a while. The cowboy did, too, but he watched her more.

She studied him back. "Don't cowboys have to get up early? You're out awful late." What was she doing? Talking to a stranger in a tavern?

But she was away from home, and everything she'd thought about herself had gone up in flames this past year. Her belly had warmed with food and the pleasant buzz of her second beer. Emily Murphy would never talk to a man in a bar—but Greg had made sure she didn't feel like Emily Murphy anymore. Changing back to her maiden name would be a formality.

And then the cowboy gave her a slow smile, and she saw the dimples that creased the leanness of his cheeks and the amusement hovering in those grass green eyes. "Yes, ma'am, it's well past my bedtime."

She bit her lip, ready to finish her burger and scurry back to her car, like the old, properly married Emily would have done. But she wasn't that person anymore. A person was made up of what she wanted, and everything Emily had thought she wanted had fallen apart. She was becoming a new woman, an independent woman, who didn't need a husband, or a mother, to make a success of her life.

But tonight, she was also just a single woman in a bar.

And who was that hurting if she was? She could smile at a man, even flirt a bit. She wasn't exactly dressed for the part, in her black sweater and jeans, but the cowboy didn't seem to mind looking at her. She felt a flush of reaction that surprised her. How long had it been since she'd felt desirable instead of just empty inside? Too long.

"You'll hear this a lot if you stick around," the cowboy continued, "but you're a stranger around here."

"Yes, I am," she said, taking the last swig of her beer. Her second beer, she thought. "I've just driven from San Francisco."

"Been here before?" he asked.

She grinned as she glanced at the mounted hunting trophies on the walls. "Not right here. But Valentine Valley? Yes, but it's been a long, long time. Since my childhood in fact. So no one will know me."

"Don't worry," he said dryly. "Everyone will make it their business to fix that."

She eased back in her chair, tilting her head as she eyed him. "You don't like that?"

He shrugged. "It's all I've ever known." Leaning his forearms on the table, he said, "Someone waiting for you tonight?"

"No." A little shiver of pleasure stirred deep in her stomach. She wouldn't let herself enjoy this too much. She was a free woman, flirting in a bar to pass the time after an exhausting day. It didn't mean anything. The bartender brought over another beer, and she didn't protest. "None of my family lives here anymore."

For a moment, the cowboy looked as if he would

question that, but instead, he glanced at the bartender. "Tony, since the dartboard's taken, mind if we use the back room?"

Emily gaped at him.

The cowboy grinned as if he could read her mind. "Pool table. Do you play?"

She giggled. Oh, she'd really had too much to drink. But it was dark and raining, and she had no family here, and no one who cared what she did. She got to her feet and grabbed her beer. "Not since college. And I was never good. But if you need a reason to stay up past your bedtime . . ."

His laugh was a pleasurable, deep rumble. As she passed his table, he stood up, and for the first time she got a good look at the size of him, the width of his shoulders thanks to whatever work he did, the flannel shirt open over a dark t-shirt, those snug jeans following long legs down to well-used cowboy boots. *Damn.* He could really work a pair of jeans. And who would have thought she'd find cowboy boots hot? She'd always been drawn to a tailored suit and the subtle hint of a well-paid profession.

The back room was deserted on this stormy night. Low central lights hung over the table, brightly illuminating the playing surface but leaving the corners of the room in the shadows. Emily set her beer down on a nearby table, and the cowboy did the same.

He chose a cue stick. As she was pulling her hair back in a quick ponytail, he turned and came to a stop, watching her. His hungry gaze traveled down her body, and though she realized her posture emphasized her breasts, she didn't stop until her hair was out of her face. It had been so long since a man looked at her with admiration and desire and need. Surely she'd be flustered—if it wasn't for the beer.

She took the cue stick from him and smiled, saying, "Thanks," knowing he'd chosen for himself.

He laughed and put several quarters in the table to release the balls. She watched him, drinking her beer and having a handful of mixed nuts from a basket on the table. Normally, she never would have eaten from food that could have been sampled by anyone. Tonight, it didn't matter. She was a new woman.

"Do you have a name, cowboy?"

He'd been leaning over the table to rack the balls, but he straightened and looked at her from beneath the brim of his hat. "Nate."

No last names. She felt a thrill of danger. "Emily."

"Pretty."

Though she normally would have blushed, this new, adventurous Emily smiled. "Thank you. But then I had no say in it."

"I wasn't talking about your name." His voice was a low drawl, his eyes narrowed and glittering.

Had it gotten warmer in here? she wondered, unable to stop looking at him. Though there were several windows, they were streaked with rain, and it would be foolish to open them. Her sweater felt like it clung to her damply.

"So, Nate," she said brightly, "are you going to take me for all my money?"

"I'm a high roller," he said. "I might bet all of a dollar."

She snorted, then covered her mouth.

"Or I might bet a kiss."

She stared at him, still smiling, playing his game and not thinking. She was so tired of thinking. "Is that the prize if I win or what I owe if I lose?"

He chuckled. "Depends, I guess. Am I worth it?"

She couldn't seem to take a deep enough breath. "I don't know. Guess we'll have to play and find out."

They didn't speak during the game, only watched each other play. Emily had to be honest with herself—she was watching him move. She liked the way his jeans tightened over his butt, how she could glimpse the muscles in his arms when he stretched out over the table. He took his hat off, and the waves in his black hair glinted under the light. The tension between them sizzled, and she wouldn't have been surprised to hear a hiss. They walked about the table, about each other, as if in a choreographed dance of evasion and teasing. This was flirtation as a high art, and he was far better at it than she'd ever been.

But the beer was helping. When it was her turn to lean over the table to line up a shot, she knew he was watching her hips, knew what, as a man, he was thinking. And although she would *never* have sex with a stranger, the thought that he desired her gave her a heady, powerful feeling. This new Emily, in the next stage of her life, could be lusty.

But not with a stranger, she reminded herself.

And then she lost the game, as she knew she would. She still had so many balls on the table as he sank his last one and slowly straightened to look at her.

"I'll take that kiss," he said, coming around the table.

Oh God. She was breathless already, looking up and up into those narrowed green eyes. He stopped right in front of her, her breasts almost touching his chest. She could feel the heat of him, the tension, the tug of danger, but it wasn't exactly him she was afraid of. She was drunk enough that she was afraid what she might do if she tasted him.

But she was also drunk enough to try it. As she stepped forward, their bodies brushed. His inhalation was sexy in itself, letting her know that she could affect him. She waited for him to lean down over her, arched her neck—and then he put his hands on her waist. She gasped as he lifted her off her feet and set her on the edge of the pool table. With wide eyes, feeling breathless, she watched him, unaware that she kept her legs pressed together until he leaned against them.

He smiled, she smiled, and then she parted her knees, holding her breath as he stepped between them. Their faces were almost level.

He leaned in and very lightly touched his lips to hers. "Breathe," he whispered, softly laughing.

She did with a sudden inhalation. What was she supposed to do with her hands? She was beginning to feel nervous and foolish and that she was making a mistake. And then he put his hands on the outside of her thighs and slowly slid them up, past the roundness of her hips to the dip in her waist.

"So delicate," he murmured huskily, and kissed her again.

Part of her had expected a drunken kiss of triumph, but he took his time, his slightly parted lips taking hers with soft, little strokes. Soon she couldn't keep herself from touching him, sliding her hands up his arms, feeling each ripple of muscle with an answering ripple of desire deep in her belly. Her thighs tightened around his hips, she slid her hands into his hair, then, as one, they deepened the kiss. He tasted of beer, and it was an aphrodisiac on this lost, lonely night. The rasp of his tongue along hers made her moan, and he pulled her tighter against him. She was lost in the heat of him, the feel of his warm, hard body in her arms. He tugged the band from her hair, and it spilled around her shoulders. She had no idea how long they kissed, only reveled in feeling absolutely wonderful. It had been so long.

He leaned over her, and she fell back, body arched beneath him, moaning again as he began to trail kisses down her jaw, then her neck. His big hands cupped her shoulders as he held her in place, her own hands clasped his head to her as if she would never let him go.

Deep inside, a whisper grew louder, that this was wrong. Another languid voice said no, they both wanted this, just a little while longer . . .

His mouth lightly touched the center V of her sweater; his hands cupped her ribs, his thumbs riding the outer curves of her breasts. The anticipation was unbearable; she wanted to writhe even as his hand slid up and over her breast as if feeling its weight. His thumb flicked across her nipple, and she jerked with pleasure. His hips were hard against hers, her legs spread to encompass him . . .

On a pool table, where anyone could walk into the back room and see them. The thrill of danger and excitement receded as guilt and worry rose up like hot bubbling water.

She was leading him on; he probably thought he could take her home and—

Torn between passion and mortification, she stiffened. "No," she whispered. Then louder, "No, please stop."

His hand froze, his head lifted until their eyes met.

She bit her lip, knowing she looked pathetic and remorseful and guilty. "I can't do this. Our bet was only for a kiss."

As he let his breath out, he straightened, pulling her up with him. He stayed between her thighs, watching her mouth. "Are you sure?" he whispered.

When she nodded, he stepped back as she jumped off the table. She stood there a moment, feeling shaky and foolish.

"I should go," she said, turning away and heading back to the bar.

At her table, she couldn't bear to wait for her bill, knowing that the bartender and the two dart players might have heard her moan. Her face was hot, her hands trembled, and she prayed that the TV had been loud enough. She threw down far more money than was probably necessary, but she just couldn't face the bartender. Grabbing her raincoat off the hook, she ran out into the rain, jumped into her car, and sat there, feeling so stupid. She'd never done anything like that in her life. That man—Nate, she remembered—must think her the worst tease.

After a minute's fumbling in the depths of her purse, she found her keys and slid them into the ignition. The car tried to turn over several times, but nothing happened. Emily closed her eyes and silently prayed. *Please, not now.*

She turned the ignition again, and although the engine strained once or twice, it wouldn't start. She stared out the rain-streaked windshield at the glowing sign for Tony's Tavern. She couldn't go back in there. Her brain was fuzzy from too much alcohol as she tried to remember what she'd driven past when she left the highway. A motel perhaps? She'd been so worried about her car and the pouring rain and her growling stomach. How far could she walk at midnight in a strange town in a storm?

With a groan, she closed her eyes, feeling moisture from the rain trickle down her neck.

An Excerpt from

TRUE LOVE AT SILVER CREEK RANCH

HER CHESTNUT QUARTER horse, Sugar, was the first to notice something wrong, startling Brooke Thalberg from her troubled thoughts. The November wind high in the Colorado Rockies, just outside Valentine Valley, was unseasonably brutal, whipping snow off the peaks of the Elk Mountains like lumbering giants exhaling icy puffs of breath. Sugar raised her head, sniffing that wind, ears twitching, leaving Brooke unsettled, uneasy, as she rode the pastures of the Silver Creek Ranch. She was checking the fence line so that the cattle didn't find their way through and wander toward someone else's land.

It was usually peaceful work, but today she was looking down the long road of her future and feeling that something was . . . wrong. And she hated to feel that way because she'd been blessed with so much.

Sugar lifted her head and shook her mane, neighing, her body tensing. Whatever she sensed wasn't going away. Brooke lifted her own head—

And smelled smoke.

A shot of fear made her vault upright in the stirrups. She scanned her family's land, focusing on the house first, framed between clusters of evergreens and aspens. But its two-story log walls seemed as sturdy as always, a faint haze of smoke rising from the stone chimney. The newer barn and sheds nearest the house seemed fine, and gradually she widened her search until she saw the old horse barn, farthest from the house—smoke billowing through the open double doors.

She kicked Sugar into a gallop, leaning forward over the horse's twitching ears, the breath frozen in her throat. *Oh, God, the horses.* Frantically, she saw that several trotted nervously around the corral as if they, too, knew something was wrong. She tried to count them, but it was as if her brain had seized with the terror of what she was seeing.

Sugar's hooves thundered beneath her, faster than even in her barrel-racing days, the ground a blur. The smoke pouring out of the open door grew darker and more menacing, twisting Brooke's fear ever higher.

At last she reached the barn and threw herself off Sugar's back, stumbling momentarily in the dirt before she found her balance. The smoke made her lungs spasm in a cough, but even that didn't make her second-guess what she had to do. She pulled her neck scarf up over the lower half of her face and ran inside, keeping to a crouch. Immediately, the world became darker as the smoke swirled around her. Her shallow breathing was hot and stifled beneath the scarf. If she let herself panic, she could become disoriented, lost, so she kept a firm grip on her emotions. She'd yet to see flames, but she could hear several horses, their neighs more like screams that tore at her heart.

"I'm coming!" she cried, flailing toward the stalls.

She ran into something hard and was only saved from falling to the ground by hands that clasped the front of her coat.

A man pulled her toward him, a stranger, tall and broad-shouldered, his face beneath his cowboy hat obscured by a scarf just like hers was. She could only see a glimpse of his narrowed, glittering eyes, focused intently on her. *Who was he? Had he set the fire?* she wondered with outrage.

"Are you all right?" He shouted to be heard above the growing roar of the fire and the frightened cries of the horses. "How many horses are there?"

For a moment, her mouth moved, and nothing came out. She saw the tack-room door hanging ajar, its interior full of fire that crackled and writhed. The sight momentarily stunned and mesmerized her, then she suddenly snapped into a sharp awareness. She couldn't worry about who this man was or what he was doing there. He'd offered to help, and that was all that mattered. Mentally, she counted the horses she'd seen out in the corral. "Should be two inside—no three!"

"I'll take that side"— he pointed through the smoke toward the west side of the barn—"and you start here."

She nodded and turned her back, beginning to fling open each stall door. At the fourth door, she was met by hooves pawing through the air. She cried out, diving sideways as they slammed into the wall right beside her. Before Dusty could rear again, she grabbed a blanket hung near the door, flung it over his head, and grabbed hold of his halter. For a moment he fought her, but she wouldn't give up.

"Please, Dusty, be a good boy. Come on!"

At last he seemed to dance toward her, and she felt a momentary triumph. She started to run, leading him toward the double doors open to the corral. As they reached fresh air, she pulled the blanket off Dusty's head and he charged to the far end, where the other horses huddled nervously.

Brooke turned around to head back into the barn, only to see the stranger leading two terrified horses outside. *Thank God*, she prayed silently. But could she have counted wrong? How could she take the chance? She tried to race past him back into the barn, but he caught her arm and wouldn't let go.

"You said three horses!" he shouted from beneath the scarf.

A groan seemed to emanate from the barn timbers, turning both their heads. Smoke wafted out in great streams to the sky, but the fire still seemed contained in the tack room.

"I can't be sure until I check each stall!" She tried to yank her elbow away, but his grip was strong. A blast of heat wafted out, engulfing her, making her sweat even more beneath her layers of winter clothing. She felt almost light-headed.

He loomed over her, and now she could see the sandy waves of hair plastered above his ears, and his narrowed eyes, brown as the sides of the barn but intent on her.

"I checked all six on the west side. I didn't hear anything more coming from the east after you'd gone."

"I can't take that chance. I only got through four stalls on my side." She stared at the herd of horses clustered uneasily at the far end of the corral. Nate's horse, Apollo—was he there? She'd never forgive herself if anything happened to him. And then she saw the dappled gray gelding, and relief shuddered down her spine.

The man didn't answer her, and she turned to see him disappear into the barn, the smoke swirling out and around him as if to draw him deep inside. A stab of fear shocked her—why was he risking himself for her? Her eyes stung as she reached the entrance, but he was there again, stumbling into her, the upper half of his face dirtied by the soot, his eyes streaming.

"It's empty!" he called.

She could have staggered with relief that her beloved horses were all right—that this brave man hadn't been injured.

But relief was only momentary as she began to think about the structure itself, built by her family well over a hundred years before. She hugged herself against the sadness.

As if reading her mind, he said, "You can't do anything now. And I hear sirens."

The fire engine from Valentine Valley roared down the dirt road that wound its way through the ranch. The horses were going to be even more frightened, so she ran to the end of the corral and opened the gate so they could escape into the next pasture.

When she returned to the stranger's side, they were pushed out of the way by the trained professionals. Most were volunteers, like Sally Gillroy from the mayor's office, who liked to gossip, and Hal Abrams, the owner of the hardware store where her dad and Nate met fellow ranchers for coffee. She recognized all these men and women, but it was strange to see their grim faces rather than easygoing smiles.

"Are you all right?" Hal demanded, his glasses reflecting the flames that had begun to shoot out both doors.

Brooke nodded, still hugging herself, feeling the presence of the stranger at her back. She almost took comfort from it, and that was strange.

"Horses all saved?"

She nodded again, and was surprised to feel a wave of pride and even excitement. Knowing she'd risked herself made her feel more alive and aware than she'd felt in a long time. Everything in life could be so transitory, and she'd just been accepting things that happened to her rather than making choices. She couldn't live that way anymore. She had to find something that made her feel this alive, that gave her more purpose and focus.

And it scared the hell out of her.

"You're in the way," Hal said. "Go on up to the house and clean up. We'll wet down any nearby buildings to keep them safe. But the barn is a goner." He turned his shrewd eyes on the stranger. "Is that blood?"

Brooke spun around and saw that the stranger had lowered his scarf. In another situation, she might have been amused at the dark upper half of his face and the white lower half, but she saw blood oozing from a cut across his cheek.

"I'm fine." The stranger used his gloved hand to swipe at his cheek and made everything worse.

"Come on," Brooke said wearily, refusing to glance one last time at her family's barn although she could hear the crackle and roar of the fire. "The bunkhouse is close. We'll wash up there and see to your face."

And she could look into his eyes and see if he was the sort who set fires for fun. He didn't seem it, for he didn't look back at the fire either, only trudged behind her.

The bunkhouse was an old log cabin, another of the original buildings from the nineteenth-century silver-boom days, when cattle from the Silver Creek Ranch had fed thousands of miners coming down from their claims to spend their riches in Valentine Valley. Brooke's father had updated the interior of the cabin to house the occasional temporary workers they needed during branding or haying season. There were a couple sets of bunk beds along the walls, an old couch before the stone hearth, a battered table and chairs, kitchen cabinets and basic appliances at the far end of the open room, and two doors that led into a single bedroom and bathroom.

The walls were filled with unframed photos of the various hands they'd employed to work the ranch over the years. Some of those photos, tacked up haphazardly and curling at the edges, were old black-and-whites going almost as far back as photography did.

Brooke shivered with a chill even as she removed her coat. The heat was only high enough to keep the pipes from freezing, and she went to raise the thermostat. When she turned around, the stranger had removed his hat and was shrugging out of his Carhartt jacket, revealing matted-down hair and a soot-stained face. He was wearing a long-sleeved red flannel shirt and jeans over cowboy boots.

To keep from staring at him, she pointed to the second door. "Go on and wash up in the bathroom. I'll find a first-aid kit."

He silently nodded and moved past her, limping slightly, shutting the door behind him. He might be hurt worse than he was saying, she thought with a wince. As she opened cabinet doors, she realized the kit was probably in the bathroom. Sighing even as she rolled up her sleeves, she let the water run in the kitchen sink until it was hot, then soaped up her black hands and started on her face. If her hair hadn't been in a long braid down her back, she'd have dunked her whole head under. She'd have to wait for a shower. Grabbing paper towels, she patted her skin dry.

A few minutes later, the stranger came out of the bathroom, his hair sticking up in short, damp curls, the first-aid kit in his hand. His face was clean now, and she could see that the two-inch cut was still bleeding.

"You probably need stitches," she said, even as the first inkling of recognition began to tease her. "You don't want a scar."

He met her gaze and held it, and she saw the faintest spark of amusement, as if he knew something she didn't.

"Don't worry about it, Brooke."

She hadn't told him her name. "So I do know you."

"It's been a long time," he said, eyeing her as openly as she was doing to him.

He was taller than her, well-muscled beneath the flannel shirt that he'd pushed up to his elbows.

And then his name suddenly echoed like a shot in her mind. "Adam Desantis," she breathed. "It's been over ten years since you went off to join the Marines."

He gave a short nod.

No wonder he looked to be in such great physical shape. Feeling awkward, she forced her gaze back to his face. He'd been good-looking in high school—and knew it—but now his face was rugged and masculine, a man grown.

She got flashes of memory then: Adam as the cool wide receiver all the high school girls wanted, with his posse of arrogant sidekicks. He'd been able to rule the school, doing whatever he wanted—because his parents hadn't cared, she reminded herself.

And then she had another memory of the sixth-grade science fair, where all the parents had helped their kids with experiments, except for his. His display had been crude and unfinished, and his mother had drunkenly told him so in front of every kid within hearing range. Whenever Brooke thought badly of his antics in high school, *that* was the memory that crept back up, making her feel ill with pity and sorrow.

"Your grandma talks about you all the time," she finally said. Mrs. Palmer spoke of him with glowing pride as he rose through the ranks to staff sergeant, a rarity at his age.

"Hope she doesn't bore everybody," he answered, showing sincerity rather than just tossing off something he didn't mean. "I hear she lives with your grandma. The Widows' Boardinghouse?"

"The name was their idea. They're kind of famous now, but those are stories for another day. Come here and let me look at your cheek." He moved toward her slowly, as if she were a horse needing to be calmed, which amused her.

"I can take care of it," he said.

"Sit down."

"I said—"

"Sit down!" She pulled out a kitchen chair and pointed. "I can't reach your face. I'm tall, but not that tall."

"Yes, ma'am," he answered gruffly.

She pressed her lips together to keep from smiling.

He eased into the chair just a touch slowly, but somehow she knew he didn't want any more questions about his health. *Adam Desantis*, she told herself again, shaking her head. He wasn't a stranger—and he wouldn't have started the fire, regardless of the trouble he'd once gotten into. She told herself to relax, but her body still tensed with an awareness that surprised her. She was just curious about him, that was all. She cleared her throat and tried to speak lightly.

"I imagine you're used to taking orders."

"Not for the last six months. I left after my enlistment was up."

Tearing open an antiseptic towelette, she leaned toward him, feeling almost nervous. Nervous? she thought in surprise. She worked what most would call a man's job and dealt with men all day. What was her problem? She got a whiff of smoke from his clothes, but his face was scrubbed clean of it. She tilted his head, her fingers touching his whisker-rough square chin, marked with a deep cleft in the center. His eyes studied her, and she was so close she could see golden flecks deep inside the brown. She stared into them, and he stared back, and in that moment, she felt a rush of heat and embarrassment all rolled together. Hoping he hadn't noticed, she began to dab at his wound, feeling him tense with the sting of the antiseptic.

Damn it all, what was wrong with her? She hadn't been attracted to him in high school—he'd been an idiot, as far as she was concerned. She'd been focused on her family ranch and barrel racing and was not the kind of girl who would lavish all her attention on a boy, as he seemed to require. Brooke always felt that she had her own life to live and didn't need a boyfriend as some kind of status symbol.

But ten years later, Adam returned as an ex-Marine who saved her horses, a man with a square-cut face, faint lines fanning out from his eyes as if he'd squinted under desert suns, and she was turning into a schoolgirl all over again.

Adam stared into Brooke Thalberg's face as she bent over him, not bothering to hide his powerful curiosity.

He remembered her, of course—who wouldn't? She was as tall as many guys and probably as strong, too, from all the hard work on her family ranch.

A brave woman, he admitted, remembering her fearlessness running into the fire, her concern for the horses more than herself. Now her hazel eyes stared at his face intently, their mix of browns and greens vivid and changeable. She turned away to search the med kit, and his gaze lingered on her slim back, covered in a checked Western shirt that was tucked in at her waist. Her long braid tumbled down her back, almost to the sway of her jeans-clad hips.

It's not like he hadn't seen a woman before. And this woman had been a pest through his childhood, too smart for her own good, seeing into his troubled life the things he'd tried to keep hidden, too confident in her own talent. She had a family who believed in her, and that gave a kid a special kind of confidence. He hadn't had that sort of family, so he recognized it when he saw it.

He wondered if she'd changed at all—he certainly had. After discovering his own confidence, he'd built a place and a name for himself in the Marines. His overconfidence had destroyed that, leaving him in a fog of uncertainty that had been hovering around him for half a year now.

Kind of like being in a barn fire, he guessed, feeling your way around, wondering if you were ever going to get out again. He still didn't know.

After using butterfly bandages to keep the wound closed, Brooke taped a small square of gauze to his face, then straightened, hands on her hips, to judge her hand-iwork. "You might need stitches if you want to avoid a scar."

He shrugged. "Got enough of those. One more won't hurt."

He rose slowly to his feet, feeling the stiffness in his leg that never quite went away. The docs had got most of the shrapnel out, but not quite all of it. The exertion of the fire had irritated the old wound, but that would ease with time. He was used to it by now, and the reminder that he was alive was more than he deserved, when there were so many men beneath the ground.

After closing the kit, Brooke turned back to face him, tilting her head to look up. They stared at each other a moment, too close, almost too intimate alone there. Drops of water still sparkled in her dark lashes, and her skin was fresh-scrubbed and free of makeup. She looked prettier than he remembered, a woman instead of the skinny girl.

Adam was surprised at the sensations her nearness inspired in him, this awareness of her as a woman, when back in high school she'd barely registered as that to him. He'd dated party girls and cheerleaders—including her best friend, Monica Shaw—not cowgirls. Now she held herself so tall and easily, with a confidence born of hard work and years of testing her body to the limits.

She cleared her throat, and her gaze dropped from his eyes to his mouth, then his shirtfront. "You have a limp," she said. "Did one of the horses kick you?"

"Had the limp on and off for a while. Nothing new."

She nodded, then stepped past him to return the med kit to the bathroom. When she came back out, she was wearing a fixed, polite smile, which, to his surprise, amused him. Not much amused him anymore.

"I'm glad you're not hurt bad," she said. "You did me—us—a big favor, and I can't thank you enough for helping rescue the horses. How'd you see the fire?"

"I was at the boardinghouse and saw the smoke out the window." If the trees hadn't been winter-bare, he might not have seen it at all, which made him think uneasily of Brooke, battling the fire alone. "Where are your brothers? They might have come in handy if I hadn't seen the fire. I assume they still work on the ranch?"

She nodded. "They're at the hospital with my dad, visiting my mom. Did you remember she has MS?"

He shook his head. "I never knew."

"She never talked about it much, so I'm not surprised. Most of the time, she only needs a cane, but she's battling a flare-up that's weakened her legs. The guys took their turn at the hospital today, while I rode fence. Guess I found more than I bargained for." She eyed him with speculation. "So you're back to visit your grandma."

She put her hands in her back pockets and rocked once on her heels, as if she didn't know what to do with herself. That stretched her shirt across her breasts, and he had to force himself to keep his gaze on her face.

"Grandma's letters were off," he admitted. "She seemed almost scattered."

Brooke focused on him with a frown. "Scattered? *Your* grandma?"

"My instincts were right. I got here, and she was a lot more frail, and she's using a cane now."

"A cane? That's new. And I see her often, so maybe I just didn't notice she'd slowly been . . ." She trailed off.

"Declining?" He almost grumbled the words. Grandma Palmer was in her seventies, but some part of him thought she never changed. She'd been the one woman who could briefly get him away from his parents to sleep on sheets that didn't smell of smoke, to eat meals that didn't come from a drive-thru. He was never hungry at Grandma Palmer's, whether for food or for love. There weren't holidays or birthdays unless Grandma had them. All he'd been to his teenage parents was an unwanted kid, the result of a broken condom, and they blamed him for making so little of their lives. He saw that now, but at the time? He'd been relieved to enlist in the Marines and start his life over.

Now he and Grandma Palmer only had each other. His parents had died after falling asleep in bed with cigarettes a few years back, and he hadn't experienced anywhere near the grief he now felt in worrying about her. He might have only seen her once or twice a year, but he'd written faithfully, and so had she. The packages she'd sent had been filled with his favorite books and food, enough to share with his buddies. He felt a spasm of pain at the memories. Some of those buddies were dead now. Good memories mingled with the bad, and he could still see Paul Ivanick cheerfully holding back Adam's care package until he promised to share Grandma Palmer's cookies.

Paul was dead now.

When Adam was discharged, it took everything in him not to run to his grandma like a little boy. But no one could make things right, not for him, or for the men who had died. The men, his Marine brothers, who were dead because of him. He didn't want to imagine what his grandma would think about him if she knew the truth.

"Those old women still seem strong," Brooke insisted. "Mrs. Ludlow may use a walker, and your grandma now a cane, but they have enough . . . well, *gumption*, to use their word, for ten women."

He shrugged. "All I know is what I see."

And then they stood there, two strangers who'd grown up in the same small town but never really knew each other.

"So what have you been up to?" Brooke asked, rocking on her heels again.

He crossed his arms over his chest. "Nothing much."

In a small town like Valentine Valley, everyone thought they deserved to know their neighbor's business. Brooke wouldn't think any different—hell, he remembered how she used to butt into his in high school, when they weren't even friends. She'd been curious about his studies, a do-gooder who thought she could change the world.

She hadn't seen the world and its cruelties, hadn't left the safety of this town, or her family, as far as he knew. *He'd* seen the world—too much of it. There was nothing he could tell her—nothing he wanted to remember.

"Oo-kay then," she said, drawing out the word.

He wondered if she felt as aware of the simmering tension between them and as uneasy as he did. He wouldn't let himself feel like this, uncertain whether he even deserved a normal life.

"What am I thinking?" she suddenly burst out, digging her hand into her pocket and coming out with a cell phone. "I haven't even called my dad."

She turned her back and stared out the window, where the firemen were hosing down the smoldering ruins of her family barn. For just a moment, Adam remembered coming to the Silver Creek Ranch as a kid when his dad would do the occasional odd jobs for the Thalbergs. He'd seen the close, teasing relationships between Brooke and her brothers, the way their parents guided and nurtured them with love. Their life had seemed so different, so foreign to him.

And now Brooke would never be able to understand the life he'd been leading. So he turned and quietly walked out the door.

About the Author

EMMA CANE grew up reading, and soon discovered that she liked to write passionate stories of teenagers in space. Her love of "passionate stories" has never gone away, although today she concentrates on the heartwarming characters of Valentine Valley, Colorado, a small town of her own creation, nestled in the Rocky Mountains.

Now that her three children are grown, Emma loves spending time crocheting and singing (although not necessarily at the same time), and hiking and snowshoeing alongside her husband, Jim, and two rambunctious dogs, Apollo and Uma.

Emma also writes *USA Today* bestselling novels under the name Gayle Callen.

Visit www.AuthorTracker.com for exclusive information on your favorite HarperCollins authors.

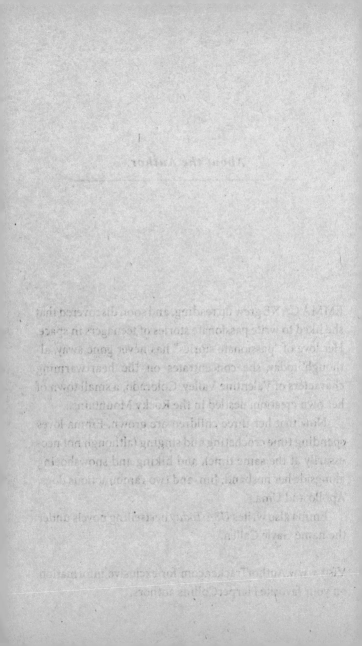

Give in to your impulses . . .
Read on for a sneak peek at four brand-new
e-book original tales of romance
from Avon Books.
Available now wherever e-books are sold.

THE CUPCAKE DIARIES:
SWEET ON YOU
By Darlene Panzera

THE CUPCAKE DIARIES:
RECIPE FOR LOVE
By Darlene Panzera

THE CUPCAKE DIARIES:
TASTE OF ROMANCE
By Darlene Panzera

ONE TRUE LOVE
A CUPID, TEXAS NOVELLA
By Lori Wilde

An Excerpt from

THE CUPCAKE DIARIES: SWEET ON YOU

by Darlene Panzera

Darlene Panzera, author of *Bet You'll Marry Me,*
launches a delicious new series that proves
business and pleasure don't mix . . . or do they?

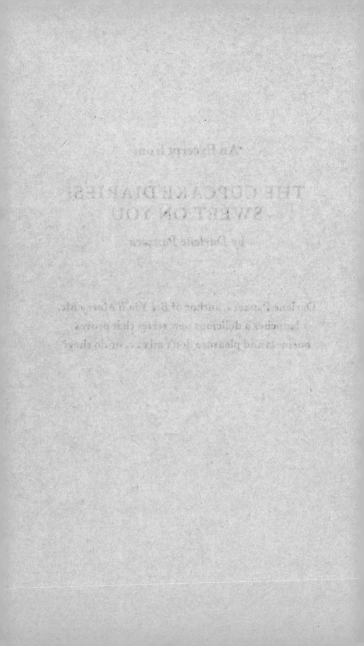

An Excerpt from

THE CUPCAKE DIARIES:
SWEET ON YOU

by Darlene Panzera

Darlene Panzera, author of *Bet You'll Marry Me*, introduces a delicious new series that proves anything is possible... if you mix it up a bit!

Andi cast a glance over the rowdy karaoke crowd to the man sitting at the front table with the clear plastic bakery box in his possession.

"What am I supposed to say?" she whispered, looking back at her dark-haired sister Kim and their redheaded friend Rachel as the three of them huddled together. " 'Can I have your cupcake?' He'll think I'm a lunatic."

"Say 'please,' and tell him about our tradition," Kim suggested.

"Offer him money." Rachel dug through her dilapidated Gucci knockoff purse and withdrew a ten-dollar bill. "And let him know we're celebrating your sister's birthday."

"You did promise me a cupcake for my birthday," Kim said with an impish grin. "Besides, the guy doesn't look like he plans to eat it. He hasn't even glanced at the cupcake since the old woman came in and delivered the box."

Andi tucked a loose strand of her dark blonde hair behind her ear and drew in a deep breath. She wasn't used to taking food from anyone. Usually she was on the other end—giving it away. Her fault. She didn't plan ahead.

Why couldn't any of the businesses here be open twenty-four hours a day, like in Portland? Out of the two dozen eclectic cafes and restaurants along the Astoria waterfront promising to satisfy customers' palates, shouldn't at least one cater to late-night customers like herself? No, they all shut down at 10:30 P.M., some earlier, as if they knew she was coming. That was what she got for living in a small town. Anticipation, but no cake.

However, she was determined not to let her younger sister down. She'd promised Kim a cupcake for her twenty-sixth birthday, and she'd try her best to procure one, even if it meant making a fool of herself.

Andi shot her ever-popular friend Rachel a wry look. "You know you're better at this than I am."

Rachel grinned. "You're going to have to start interacting with the opposite sex again sometime."

Maybe. But not on the personal level Rachel's tone suggested. Andi's divorce the previous year had left behind a bitter aftertaste that no amount of sweet talk could dissolve.

Pushing back her chair, Andi stood up. "Tonight, all I want is the cupcake."

Andi had taken only five steps when the man with the bakery box turned his head and smiled.

He probably thought she was coming over hoping to find

a date. Why shouldn't he? The Captain's Port was filled with people looking for a connection. If not for a lifetime, then at least for the few hours they shared within the friendly confines of the restaurant's casual, communal atmosphere.

She hesitated mid-step before continuing forward. Heat rushed into her cheeks. Dressed in jeans and a navy blue tie and sportcoat jacket, he was even better looking than she'd first thought. Thirtyish. Light brown hair, fair skin, sparkling chocolate brown eyes. *Oh, my.* He could have his pick of any girl in the place. Any girl in Astoria, Oregon.

"Hi," he greeted.

Andi swallowed the nervous tension gathering at the back of her throat and managed a smile in return. "Hi. I'm sorry to bother you, but it's my sister's birthday, and I promised her a cupcake." She nodded toward the see-through box and waved the ten-dollar bill. "Is there any chance I can persuade you to sell the one you have here?"

The guy's brows shot up. "You want my cupcake?"

An Excerpt from

THE CUPCAKE DIARIES: RECIPE FOR LOVE

by Darlene Panzera

In the second installment of Darlene Panzera's
new series, another Creative Cupcakes
founder discovers that a little magic may be
the secret ingredient in the recipe for love.

Rachel pushed through the double doors of the kitchen, took one look at the masked man at the counter, and dropped the tray of fresh-baked cupcakes on the floor.

Did he plan to rob Creative Cupcakes? Demand she hand over the money from the cash register? Her eyes darted around the frilly pink-and-white cupcake shop. The loud clang of the metal bakery pan hitting the tile had caused several customers sitting at tables to glance in her direction. Would the masked man threaten the other people as well? How could she protect them?

She stepped over the white-frosted chocolate mess by her feet, tried to judge the distance to the telephone on the wall, and turned her attention back to the masked man before her. Maybe he wasn't a robber, but someone dressed for a costume party or play. The man with the black masquerade mask covering the upper half of his face also wore a black cape.

"If this is a holdup, you picked the wrong place, Zorro." She tossed her fiery red curls over her shoulder with false bravado and laid a protective hand across the old bell-ringing register. "We don't have any money."

His hazel eyes sparkled through the holes in the mask, and he flashed her a disarming smile. "Maybe I can help with that."

He turned his hand to show an empty palm, and relief flooded over her. No gun. Then he closed his fingers and swung his fist around in the air three times. When he opened his palm again, he held a quarter, which he tossed her way.

Rachel caught the coin and laughed. "You're a magician."

"Mike the Magnificent," he said, extending his cape wide with one arm and taking a bow. "I'm here for the Lockwell party?"

Rachel pointed at the door leading to the back party room. The space had originally been a tattoo shop, but the tattoo artist had relocated to the rental next door. "The Lockwells aren't here yet. The party doesn't start until three."

"I came early to set up before the kids arrive," Mike told her. "Can't have them discovering my secrets."

"No, I guess not," Rachel agreed. "If they did, Mike the magician might not be so magnificent."

"Magnificence is hard to maintain." His lips twitched as if he were suppressing a grin. "Are you Andi?"

She shook her head. "Rachel, Creative Cupcakes' stupendous co-owner, baker, and promoter."

This time a grin *did* escape his mouth, which led her to notice his strong, masculine jawline.

"Tell me, Rachel, what is it that makes you so stupendous?"

She gave him her most flirtatious smile. "Sorry, I can't reveal my secrets, either."

"Afraid if I found out the truth I might not think you were so impressively great?"

Rachel froze, fearing Mike the magician might be a mind reader as well. Careful to keep her smile intact, she forced herself to laugh off his comment.

"I just don't think it's nice to brag," she responded playfully.

"Chicken," he taunted in an equally playful tone, making his way toward the party room door.

Despite the uneasy feeling he'd discovered more about her in three minutes than most men did in three years, she wished he'd stayed to chat a few minutes more.

Andi Burke, wearing one of the new, hot pink Creative Cupcakes bibbed aprons, came in from the kitchen and stared at the cupcake mess on the floor. "What happened here?"

"Zorro came in, gave me a panic attack, and the tray slipped out of my hands." Rachel grabbed a couple paper towels and squatted down to scoop up the crumpled cake and splattered frosting before her OCD-about-kitchen-safety friend could comment further. "Don't worry, I'll take care of the mess."

"I should have told you Officer Lockwell hired a magician for his daughter's birthday party." Andi bent to help her, and, when they stood back up, asked, "Did you speak to Mike?"

Rachel nodded, her gaze on the door to the party room as it opened and Mike reappeared.

Tipping his head toward them as he walked across the shop, he said, "Good afternoon, ladies."

An Excerpt from

THE CUPCAKE DIARIES:
TASTE OF ROMANCE

by Darlene Panzera

In the final installment of Darlene Panzera's
charming series, one lonely cupcake decorator
will learn that love is worth the risk . . .
once she gets a little taste of romance.

Focus, Kim reprimanded herself. *Keep to the task at hand and stop eavesdropping on other people's conversations.*

But she didn't need to hear the crack of the teenage boy's heart to feel his pain. Or to remember the last time she'd heard the wretched words, *"I'm leaving"* spoken to her.

She tried to ignore the couple as she picked up the pastry bag filled with pink icing and continued to decorate the tops of the strawberry preserve cupcakes. However, the discussion between the high school boy and the young woman she assumed to be his girlfriend kept her ears attentive.

"When will I see you again?" the boy asked.

Kim glanced toward them, leaned closer, and held her breath.

"I don't know," the girl replied.

The soft lilt in her accent thrust the familiarity of the conversation even deeper into Kim's soul.

"I'm going to the university for two years," the girl continued. "Maybe we'll meet again after."

Not likely. Kim shook her head, and the bottom of her stomach locked down tight. From past experience, she knew that once the school year was over in June, most foreign students went home, never to return.

And left many broken hearts in their wake.

"Two years is a long time," the boy said.

Forever is even longer. Kim drew in a deep breath as the unmistakable catch in the poor boy's voice replayed again and again in her mind. And her heart.

How long were they going to stand there and torment her by reminding her of her parting four years earlier with Gavin, the Irish student she'd dated in college? Dropping the bag of icing on the Creative Cupcakes counter, she moved toward them.

"Can I help you?" Kim asked, pulling on a new pair of food handler's gloves.

"I'll have the white chocolate macadamia," the girl said, pointing to the cupcake she wanted in the glass display case.

The boy dug his hands into his pockets, counted the meager change he'd managed to withdraw, and turned five shades of red.

"None for me." His Adam's apple bobbed as he swallowed. "How much for hers?"

"You have to have one, too," the girl protested. "It's your birthday."

Kim took one look at his lost-for-words expression and took pity on him. "If today is your birthday, the cupcakes are free," she said. "For both you and your guest."

The teenage boy's face brightened. "Really?"

Kim nodded and removed the cupcakes the two lovebirds wanted from the display case. She even put a birthday candle on one of them. A heart on the other. Maybe the girl would come back for him. Or he would fly to Ireland for her. *Maybe*.

Her eyes stung, and she squeezed them shut for a brief second. When she opened them again, she set her jaw. Enough was enough. Now that they had their cupcakes, she could escape back into her work and forget about romance and relationships and every regrettable moment she'd ever wasted on love.

She didn't need it. Not like her older sister, Andi, who'd recently lost her heart to Jake Hartman, their Creative Cupcakes financer and a news writer for the *Astoria Sun*. Or like her other co-owner friend, Rachel, who'd just gotten engaged to Mike Palmer, a miniature model maker for movies who also doubled as the driver of their Cupcake Mobile.

All she needed was to dive deep into her desire to put paint on canvas. She glanced at the walls of the cupcake shop, adorned with her scenic oil, acrylic, and watercolor paintings. Maybe if she worked hard enough, she'd have the money to open her own art gallery and she wouldn't need to decorate cupcakes anymore.

But for now, she needed to serve the next customer.

An Excerpt from

ONE TRUE LOVE
A Cupid, Texas Novella
by Lori Wilde

Find out how the magic behind *New York Times*
bestselling author Lori Wilde's Cupid, Texas
series began with this heartwarming
story of a love that inspired a legend.

Whistle Stop, Texas
May 25th, 1924

I met John Fant on the worst day of my life.

There he was, the most handsome man I'd ever seen, standing at the bottom of my daddy's porch clutching a straw Panama hat in his hand, the mournful expression on his face belying the jauntiness of his double-breasted lightweight jacket and Oxford bags with sharp, smart creases running smoothly down the fronts of the legs. An intense, magnetic energy radiated from him, rolled toward me like heat waves off the Chihuahuan Desert. I felt an inexplicable tug square in the center of my belly.

His gaze settled heavily on my face. There were shadows under his eyes, as if he'd been up all night, and there was a tightness to his lips that troubled me. A snazzy red Nash

Roadster sat on a patch of dirt just off the one-lane wagon road that ran in front of the house. It looked just as out of place as the magnificent man in my front yard.

My knees turned as watery as the mustang grape jelly I'd canned the summer before that hadn't set up right, and suddenly I couldn't catch my breath. I hung onto the screen door that I was half hiding behind.

"Is this Corliss Greenwood's residence?" he asked.

"Yessir." I raised my chin and stepped out onto the porch. The screen door wavered behind me, the snap stretched out of the spring from too many years of too many kids slamming it closed. Without looking around, I kicked the door shut with my bare heel.

He came up on the porch, the termite-weakened steps sagging and creaking underneath his weight.

Shame burned my cheeks. *Please, God, don't let him put one of those two-tone wingtips right through a rotten board.*

He was tall, with broad shoulders, and even though he was whip-lean, he looked as strong as a prizewinning Longhorn bull. A spot of freshly dried blood stained his right cheek where he must have cut himself shaving. He'd shaved in the middle of the day, in the middle of the week? His hair was the color of coal, and he wore it slicked back off his forehead. His teeth were straight and white as piano keys, and I imagined that when he smiled, it went all the way up to his chocolate brown eyes. But he wasn't smiling now.

Mr. Fant had caught me indisposed. I must have looked frightful in the frayed gray dress I wore when cleaning. The material was way too tight around my chest because my breasts had blossomed along with the spring flowers. Strands of unruly hair were popping out of my sloppy braid and falling around my face. I pushed them back.

Another step closer and he was only an arm's length away.

My heart started thudding. His masculine fragrance wafted over to me in the heat of the noonday sun, notes of leather, oranges, rosemary, cedar, clove, and moss. Perfume! He was wearing perfume. I'd never met a man who wore perfume before, but it smelled mighty good, fresh and clean and rich.

My daddy always said I would have made a keen bloodhound with the nose I had on me. A well-developed sense of smell can be good for some things, like telling when a loaf of warm yeast bread is ready to come out of the oven, and inhaling a snout full of sunshine while unpinning clothes from the line, but other times having a good sniffer can be downright unpleasant—for instance, when visiting the outhouse in August.

"Is Corliss your father?"

My throat had squeezed up, so I just nodded.

"I'm John Fant."

I knew who he was, of course. The Fants were the wealthiest family in Jeff Davis County. Truth be told, they were the wealthiest family between the Pecos River and the New Mexico border. The Fants had founded the town of Cupid, which lay twenty-five miles due north in the Foothills of the Fort Davis Mountains, and they owned the Fant Silver Mine, where my father worked. Three years before, when John had returned home with a degree from Maryland State College, his father, Silas Fant, had turned the family business over to his only son.

The screen door drifted open against my calf, and I bumped it closed again.

He arched a dark eyebrow. "And you are . . . ?"

"Millie Greenwood." I barely managed to push my name over my lips.